And what ... you feeling?

She hadn't expected that question to come up, not where Trey was concerned. This was a business proposition, pure and simple, and feelings shouldn't have come into it at all. But now that the line had been crossed between business and emotion...she had to admit she wasn't quite sure what she was feeling. She was irritated at him for taking advantage of the situation, that was for sure. Intrigued by what on earth his reasons could be. Fascinated at what he might be plotting. Annoyed at...

Time was what she needed, to sort everything out in her head and decide what to do. Time to think about the situation, and about what she wanted, and about Trey.

Especially about Trey, a little voice whispered in the back of her mind.

Darcy did her best to ignore it.

From city girl—to corporate wife!

Working side by side, nine to five—and beyond....
No matter how hard these couples try to keep their
relationships strictly professional, romance is
definitely on the agenda!

But will a date in the office diary lead to
an appointment at the altar?

Next month, look out for
Contracted: Corporate Wife
by Jessica Hart,
Harlequin Romance #3861

Leigh Michaels wrote her first book when she was
fourteen and thought she knew everything. Now she's
a good bit older, and wise enough to realize that she'll
never know everything. She has written more than
75 romance novels, teaches writing in person and
online, and enjoys long walks, miniatures and watching
wild deer and turkey from her living room.

Leigh loves to hear from readers. You may contact her
at: P.O. Box 935, Ottumwa, Iowa 52501, U.S.A. or visit
her Web site: leigh@leighmichaels.com

Books by Leigh Michaels

HARLEQUIN ROMANCE®
3815—THE HUSBAND SWEEPSTAKE
3836—ASSIGNMENT: TWINS

THE CORPORATE MARRIAGE CAMPAIGN

Leigh Michaels

TORONTO • NEW YORK • LONDON
AMSTERDAM • PARIS • SYDNEY • HAMBURG
STOCKHOLM • ATHENS • TOKYO • MILAN • MADRID
PRAGUE • WARSAW • BUDAPEST • AUCKLAND

ISBN 0-373-03857-7

THE CORPORATE MARRIAGE CAMPAIGN

First North American Publication 2005.

Copyright © 2005 by Leigh Michaels.

www.eHarlequin.com

Printed in U.S.A.

CHAPTER ONE

THE sound of a key clicking in the lock roused Darcy just enough to make her moan and turn over, but not enough to make her aware of where she was—which was why, when Dave came through the front door a few seconds later, she was sprawled on the carpet next to the couch she'd just fallen from.

Dave stopped dead, his briefcase still swinging. "What are you doing down here?"

Darcy rubbed her neck. "Sleeping, apparently."

"Was it too stuffy for you upstairs last night? Maybe we need to put an air conditioner in."

"As far as I know, it's fine. I haven't been up there."

Dave raised an eyebrow. "Are you nursing a hangover?"

"No, David—not unless they've started putting something alcoholic into tea bags." Darcy pushed herself up into a sitting position against the front of Mrs. Cusack's desk. It was plenty solid enough to lean against; there was no chance that the massive desk would slide out from behind her. "I finished up a dozen job applications—they're right there, all ready to mail—and the last thing I remember, I sat down for a minute on the couch to admire the stack. I must have been more tired than I thought."

"How late were you up?"

Darcy shrugged. "I remember noticing 3:00 a.m., but I was still making copies then so it must have been a lot later when I actually crashed." She gave an enormous yawn and grumbled, "This isn't fair, you know. If I'm going to wake up with the same symptoms as a hangover, I should at least have the fun of a party to remember. I'm going to bed."

"Uh, Darcy…"

"I don't like the sound of that, Dave."

"Mrs. Cusack called me at home this morning. She isn't going to be coming in today, so I wondered if you could fill in."

"Again? I suppose her sinuses are still acting up."

"I told her it would be all right, because you'd be here. Sorry."

"Does it appear to you that ever since I came back to town, your secretary has gotten into the habit of calling in sick a couple of times a week? That's not a complaint, by the way, just a comment."

"She thinks you're taking advantage of me, living rent free in the penthouse."

The penthouse. It was Darcy herself who had named it that, back when Dave had bought the little cottage to house his fledgling law practice and moved into the half-finished attic in order to ease the strain on his finances. She hadn't expected then that she'd ever be living there herself, even temporarily.

"Well, it's not exactly the Ritz—but whatever Mrs. Cusack thinks, I appreciate having the accommodations." Darcy shook her head, trying to clear it. "And I'm happy to lend a hand. I'll pull myself together here in a minute, but some coffee would sure help."

"I'll start a pot."

"Well, go easy on it. The battery acid you call coffee—"

"It's guaranteed to wake you up."

"David, your coffee would wake up a corpse. Do I have time for a shower? Not that you want me greeting clients without one, after I worked most of the night."

Dave checked his wristwatch. "I'm not expecting anybody for an hour or so. If you like, I'll make sure the hot water runs out before then so you won't be walking through the waiting room wearing a towel."

"That's such a comfort. So generous of you to help me out." Darcy pushed herself up from the floor and headed across the minuscule hallway to the cottage's single bathroom. "Though the way I feel at the moment, a cold shower might be a better idea."

She stayed under the spray as long as she dared, then wrapped her hair in a towel and slid reluctantly back into her sweats. Where was her brain, anyway, that she hadn't run upstairs for some fresh clothes before she stripped off?

It was going to be another long day, she reflected. But with her applications finished, she really had nothing else to do but mail them and start assembling the next list of potential jobs. Staying busy with Dave's clients and paperwork was better than having too much time to think about her own situation, anyway.

And it felt good to be able to help Dave out a bit in return for all he was doing for her right now. The penthouse might not quite match up to its grandiose name, but it was a place to sleep and store her stuff till she got herself established again. And since he'd refused to even consider charging her rent, the least she could do was pitch in around the office. Once this was over—as soon as she had a job again, and her own place, and a bank account—she'd do something really nice for Dave...

She was so absorbed in her thoughts that she had walked halfway through the waiting room toward the stairs before she realized that a man and a woman were standing in the center of the room, looking around as if they felt lost.

Had she been in the shower that long? Surely not, because Dave hadn't been kidding about the hot water supply. So either his clients had arrived far earlier than their appointment, or this was an unexpected addition to his day. Did he even realize they were here? If they'd just walked in, and he hadn't heard the door...

"Hi," she said. "Can I help you?"

The man turned to face her. His raised eyebrows said that he doubted very much that she could be of any assistance at all. No surprise there, Darcy thought. In her baggy, mismatched sweats, stained with india ink and acrylic paint, with her hair piled in a makeshift turban, she no doubt looked more like the cleaning lady than the confidential secretary she was supposed to be today.

Especially in comparison to his own elegant good looks. He was made for a courtroom, she thought—tall, broad-shouldered, dark haired, with a profile that looked as if it had been chiseled by a Renaissance master and a pin-striped suit that could have been fitted by the same loving touch. He was looking down his classic nose at her, obviously waiting for her to justify her existence.

Well, it was all right with Darcy if Mr. Elegance found her unappealing. She'd had her fill of guys who were gorgeous and knew how to use their looks to advantage. Packaging wasn't everything.

"You've taken us a bit off guard this morning, I'm afraid," she said. "We weren't expecting you."

"I phoned right before we came over," he said curtly.

The voice matched the rest of him, Darcy thought—deep and rich but with a hard edge.

That's great, she thought. He must have talked to Dave while she was in the shower, and now Darcy looked like either a liar or an idiot. *Where do we go from here?*

She let her gaze drift from the man to his companion, and blinked in surprise. Who went out in public these days wearing a black picture hat with a heavy veil? Grieving widows? Movie stars? Someone who had no idea what a cliché she was wearing?

Even more surprising, Darcy thought, was why hadn't she noticed that attention-grabbing hat before now. Surely it should have jumped out at her the instant she laid eyes on the couple. Not that Mr. Elegance wasn't worth looking at all by himself—but it almost seemed as if he'd been trying to get in the way, as if he'd been deliberately trying to block her view of his feminine companion.

Dave called from the kitchen, "I've got it, Darcy. Just as soon as I get the coffee poured I'll be in. Show them into my office, will you?"

Darcy took a step back and with a purposely theatrical gesture invited the couple toward the back of the house, where Dave had converted one of the cottage's original bedrooms into his office.

If he'd been expecting clients, it wasn't obvious—at least, the clutter looked just the same to Darcy as it had yesterday. Dave had dropped his briefcase into one of the two chairs supposedly reserved for clients, just as he usually did. Darcy fished it out and set it atop a pile of law books on the credenza, and then tried to clear off enough space on the desk so he could set down a tray.

Just yesterday, she remembered, she'd told Dave that he should rearrange the front room—currently the law library—enough to put in a desk. That would create a public office, an attractive and restful place to meet with his clients away from the disorder of his working desk. He'd told her that the clients he was most interested in didn't mind untidiness, and Darcy hadn't argued the point because on second thought she'd realized it would only give him another flat surface to fill with clutter.

Dave came in carrying not a tray but three foam cups, full to the brim with steaming and very black coffee. That was Dave, she thought—straightforward and without an ounce of pretension.

She wondered what Mr. Elegance thought of the service, and shot a look at him from the corner of her eye. "David, perhaps your guests would like cream and sugar?'' she suggested gently.

"Trey doesn't use it," Dave said. "But I don't know…" His gaze rested on the woman in the hat. He looked worried.

"Cream, please," she said softly. "I don't think I can drink it so hot."

"Would you get the cream, Darcy?" Dave asked. "But first let me introduce you. This is Trey—"

"Smith," Mr. Elegance said.

Darcy was still watching Dave, feeling bemused by the concern in his face as he looked at the mysterious lady under the picture hat, and she saw his eyes widen ever so slightly. Someone who didn't know him well might not even have realized he was startled, but Darcy wasn't fooled. Dave's client was lying, and Dave knew it.

Of course, who wouldn't be suspicious? *Smith*… Honestly, couldn't the man come up with a better alias than that?

"Nice to meet you, Mr. Smith," Darcy said dryly. "We get so many of those among our clientele, I hope you won't mind if I have trouble keeping you straight from all the others. And Mrs. Smith, I presume?"

"Come on, Trey," Dave said. "This is my sister Darcy. She's helping out on short notice today because my secretary's sick."

Mr. Elegance—or Smith—looked Darcy over from head to toe.

She'd never felt more like a dust mop in her life. Which was a ridiculous reaction, she told herself. Just because he was beautifully attired in a hand-tailored suit didn't give him any right to judge her costume. "Actually," she confided, "I dress this way because it makes the criminal element among our clients feel right at home. I was going to wear my Property Of Cook County Jail jumpsuit today, but

I'm afraid it's in the laundry. If you'll excuse me, I'll go get the cream.''

The cream was at the back of the refrigerator, still in the big plastic supermarket jug, and of course, she couldn't find anything to serve it in. If Dave had ever owned a cream and sugar set, she couldn't remember seeing it, and the only alternative was yet another of the ubiquitous foam cups. And of course she couldn't find a tray. So she put the cream jug and the sugar canister on a pizza pan, along with a couple of spoons and the last of a package of paper napkins she found crumpled in the back of a drawer.

She was just starting through the cottage toward the office when Dave called, ''Darcy! Bring some ice, too!''

Ice? What next? With any luck, Darcy decided, she might manage to get upstairs to dress sometime before noon.

At least there was an ice bucket—which she supposed said something about Dave's priorities, or perhaps those of his clients. She tipped out the receipts which had collected in the bucket onto the kitchen counter, rinsed it out and froze her fingers dipping cubes from the ice maker.

''Isn't it a little early for cocktails?'' she asked as she backed into the office.

Then she saw why Dave had wanted ice, and she almost dropped the pizza pan.

The mysterious woman in the picture hat was mysterious no longer. At least, she wasn't hiding her identity anymore, though Darcy would bet there was quite a story behind the blackened eye, the bruised jaw, and the angry-looking cut on her upper lip. No wonder the woman had said she couldn't drink her coffee hot.

Darcy set the pizza pan atop Dave's desk, pushed the cream and sugar off the dish towel she'd used to cover up the discolored surface of the pan, dumped the ice into the towel, and held it out to the blonde. "Car accident?" she said. "Or—something else?"

"Something else," the blonde said. "Thanks." She cradled the towel against her cheek.

Mr. Elegance held out a hand. "I'm Trey Kent," he said gruffly. "This is my sister Caroline. Dave assures me you're able to keep a secret—and now you know why I was concerned about that."

"Yes," Darcy said. "If I can help in any way—"

"That's what we're here to discuss with Dave," Trey said.

Dismissed. Darcy felt like saluting.

They were still behind closed doors when she came back downstairs a few minutes later, dressed in heather tweed slacks and a short-sleeved sweater. She was leaning over Mrs. Cusack's desk, reviewing the day's calendar, when she heard the doorknob of Dave's office give its characteristic groan, and she pushed the calendar aside and hurried toward the kitchen to make another pot of coffee.

Not, she told herself, to avoid coming face to face with Mr. Elegance again. She couldn't possibly care less what he thought about her.

The telltale loose board in the hallway creaked, and a moment later Trey Kent was standing in the kitchen doorway, the sopping-wet towel in his hand. He was holding it gingerly, as if afraid it would drip on his perfectly creased trousers. "I think we're finished with this, Ms. Malone."

Darcy took the towel, wrung it out, and hung it over the faucet. "I hope it helped."

"You were very kind."

She waited for him to go back to Dave's office, but instead he leaned against the front of the cabinets and folded his arms across his chest. "My sister's wedding is scheduled for the middle of December."

And why are you telling me about it? "Really? Now that

just goes to show why Dave's the lawyer and I'm the part-time secretary, because I'd have guessed she was here for a restraining order, not a prenuptial contract. Unless of course it wasn't the fiancé who did this to her.''

"It was. And she won't be marrying him.''

"Well, that's good news. Most battered women are so off balance about the whole thing that they blame themselves for getting beaten—and they don't even consider filing charges.''

"Can you blame them? Taking the whole thing to court is complicated, inconvenient, unpleasant and time-consuming.''

Darcy looked at him thoughtfully. "Don't forget *embarrassing*,'' she said coolly. "Especially for the family.''

"Not to mention risky for the victim who stands up against an abuser.''

"So is that why she's talking to Dave instead of the district attorney—because you'd rather handle it all quietly?''

"Not quite. We have an appointment with the district attorney later this morning, but I brought Caroline to see Dave first so he could tell her why it's absolutely necessary she not back down and let Corbin go free to do it again to someone else. But I'm sure you don't need the legal process explained to you.''

Darcy bit her lip. "Oh. I thought—''

"It was quite clear what you thought, Ms. Malone. In the meantime, however, this whole thing has left us with a problem.''

"*Us?*'' Darcy asked. "I assume you're speaking generically, because I don't feel that this is exactly a personal difficulty for me.''

"A problem for Caroline and for me. And for the Kentwells chain.''

Darcy snapped her fingers. "Of course. Kentwells—the

department store group. No wonder your name sounded familiar. Trey Kent...let me think. You're not actually named Trey, are you? You're Something, Something Kent the Third—that's where they got the Trey.''

"It's better than being called Junior as my father sometimes was."

"No contest there. So what is your name, really?"

"Andrew Patrick Kent." He added, sounding reluctant, "The Third."

"All those nice first names and you don't use a single one of them. Such a shame."

"Has your brother ever told you you're impertinent?"

"Frequently. But since I'm not officially working for him, he can't fire me, you see."

"He said you're not working at all right now."

"On the contrary." Darcy reached for a mug. "I'm working very hard to get a full-time job. In fact, one of the applications in the stack on the desk, waiting for the mailman to pick it up, is addressed to the head of marketing at the Kentwells stores. I put my best samples in it. Of course, I put my best samples in all the packages I send out."

"Marketing," he said thoughtfully. "Dave said you're trained as a graphic artist."

"You know, it sounds to me as if Dave was doing more talking about me than about his client. That's not like Dave."

His gaze flickered. "I asked him about you."

"Really? I don't suppose you'd care to tell me why you wanted to know?"

"I might be able to pull some strings for you."

"Why would you want to?" Darcy asked bluntly. "Why would it even occur to you? The impression I made this morning can't have been anything to make you want to help me out. Or do you mean Dave asked you to give me a hand?"

He didn't answer. "You have a certain potential."

"Oh, I get it. You'll find me a job with your competitors so I can create chaos for them. Or are you just interested in getting me out of here so I can't gossip about Caroline's problems? Of course it's a little late to prevent me from talking about what happened this morning, if I wanted to. Not that I would, because I can keep a secret."

"Dave assures me you're the soul of discretion." His voice was dry.

"But you don't believe him, so you want to cut a private deal to keep me from blowing my mouth off."

He didn't answer. "I'd like to tell you about my problem, Ms. Malone. Or may I call you Darcy?"

"I guess I can't stop you from calling me whatever you want. But before you tell me all the gory details about Caroline, you should know I don't counsel battered women or the guys who beat them up."

"I have no intention of telling you the details, gory or otherwise, about Caroline."

"Then what on earth can I do for you, Trey?"

He seemed to flinch at the name. Darcy had expected he would, and that was exactly why she'd used it.

"I started to tell you earlier," he pointed out. "If I might finish my explanation?"

Darcy handed him a mug of coffee. "Sure. I've got nothing to do but listen."

"When Caroline first set her wedding date, the stores' advertising department decided to take advantage of the fact. What they came up with is a sort of hybrid of royal wedding and advertising blitz."

"Interesting combination."

"They've planned a three-month-long program of print and media ads showing the bride and groom choosing everything for their wedding and their new home."

"From an engagement ring to a lawnmower," Darcy murmured.

"I don't think they thought of the lawnmower."

"Then your advertising department is obviously in need of some fresh blood."

He winced.

"Sorry," Darcy murmured. "I guess that's probably not a good image right now, considering Caroline's bruises and that scab on her lip."

"At any rate, the ad space and time have already been scheduled, the merchandise which will be featured has all been selected, and the photographers are booked to take the pictures. In fact, they started two days ago."

"I begin to see the dimensions of the problem," Darcy murmured. "You've got all the pieces of a campaign and now the stars have winked out on you."

"That's about the size of it."

Darcy sipped her coffee. "I don't suppose you could be lucky enough that the fight between Caroline and her fiancé was over another man? Then you could just blot out the current guy from the photos and substitute the head of the new one."

"No," he said. "We'll have to start over."

"Of course you'll have Caroline's split lip to contend with—though I suppose you could photograph her only in profile, until she heals…"

"Are you always this irreverent?"

"Generally, yes," Darcy admitted. "Though perhaps I should point out that it isn't my intention to be disrespectful to Caroline and the trouble she's having." *Only to you. Why are you telling me all this, anyway—Mr. Smith who wanted so badly to be anonymous?*

"Dave suggested we use someone else."

"You know," Darcy murmured, "I'm always amazed

when it's the expensive attorney who comes up with the obvious answer and thinks it's brand-new and original.''

''Yes, I'd already considered the possibility of making a switch. The question, of course, is who to use instead.''

Darcy shrugged. ''Doesn't the store have a bridal registry? You could call up the couples who are already listed and ask if they'd like some free stuff in return for using their pictures.''

''Those people are already well into the process. They've made most of their decisions already. The whole point of the campaign is the excitement when a bride and groom look at all the options the store makes available to them.''

''And then they're going to choose exactly the merchandise you've already decided to feature? Sorry, I suppose I'm being irreverent again.''

''Plus we need to start shooting again tomorrow—we're already well behind schedule—and that doesn't leave time to do background checks on the people who are already listed in the bridal registry.''

''Investigate them? Whatever for?''

''Considering why I'm here this morning, I'm surprised you have to ask. We narrowly escaped putting a batterer into a prominent spot in our advertising. I'd hate to find out after the fact that we chose a bigamist or a sex offender instead.''

''You're just about as big a cynic as Dave is. Okay, how about Dave?''

''Dave?''

''Salt of the earth. He wouldn't exactly be royal wedding material, but the ads would have the advantage of looking like real people.''

''Real people?''

''Yes. Pardon me for saying it, but I think the average customer of your department store is likely to have a little trouble picturing herself in Caroline's size three bikini.

Your sister's gorgeous—or she would be without the bruises. But she looks like a model. Whereas if you had a normal-size, normal-looking bride and groom—''

"Someone like Dave."

"Sure. Why not ask him how he feels about it?"

"I did. He said he was more accustomed to dealing with mopping up the other end of a marriage."

"How long have you known him, anyway? Surely it doesn't surprise you that he's a bit jaded after all the divorces he's handled. Maybe he just needs a little encouragement to settle down. Give him a nice gift package, a little publicity for the law practice..."

"He also said he wasn't dating anyone."

"Now, that's malarkey. He's always dating someone. The current girlfriend called here last night, as a matter of fact. Which reminds me—I forgot to tell him that Ginger phoned."

"Yes," Trey said dryly. "I see now why you said you're good at keeping a secret."

Darcy made a face at him. "The point is, if he told you he wasn't dating anyone, he was pulling your leg."

"You didn't let me finish. Actually, what he said was that he wasn't dating anyone he would consider for an instant in connection with the word 'bride.'"

Darcy blinked in surprise. "Now that makes me feel a little crazy. He harped at me all the way through college about how I should never even go out for a slice of pizza with a guy I wouldn't consider marrying. Now he's dating someone he himself thinks is inappropriate—''

"I thought you said you'd talked to her. She must not be so bad if you think she's all right."

"Well, I've only been back in town for a week, so I haven't actually met her. Now I can't wait to see what he means."

He shifted restlessly against the cabinets. "If we could stay on topic, Darcy."

"Oh. Sure. Well, if you can't find a bride and groom, you could always turn the whole thing into a public service campaign to promote awareness of domestic violence." Belatedly, Darcy remembered the picture hat, the veil, the alias. "Though I guess Caroline wouldn't want to go quite that public, right?"

"There would also be a little matter of slander if her ex-fiancé's name came into it."

"Technically, slander doesn't apply—not if you're telling the truth. At least, I think that's the case, but maybe you should ask Dave about slander and libel."

"I don't need to. After the trial is over, Caroline can be the poster child for battered women if she chooses—but in the meantime, I still have a problem."

"Well, Dave's very resourceful. I'm sure he'll think of something."

"He has thought of something. Me."

Darcy wondered why that particular solution hadn't occurred to her. Not because she'd assumed someone like Trey Kent was already taken, because that possibility hadn't even crossed her mind. There was an air of independence around him which said that no woman—other than perhaps Caroline—had a say in what he did. But it was odd how she'd known that without even stopping to think about it.

"Well, it's not exactly a unique solution," Darcy mused, "but it works. Marry off the prince instead of the princess. After all, one royal wedding is pretty much like another. And for the good of the store, surely a little thing like getting married probably wouldn't be any big deal to you at all. Problem solved. More coffee?"

"I have no intention of getting married."

"Oh? What have you got against marriage?"

"Nothing in particular. I just wasn't planning to walk down the aisle anytime soon."

"So you're just going to play the part? If that's all it takes, then why not hire actors?"

"You said yourself it would be much more believable if the models were real people."

"Well, yes, it would. But isn't it a little shady to pretend?"

"Who does it hurt?" Trey asked coolly. "The only difference is that on the last page, the happy couple will ride off into the sunset separately instead of together."

"You'll keep up the fiction all the way?"

"Right up to the end of the campaign—and then cut, stop the action. It won't matter to the customer who's looked at the ads. She's already had her thrills along the way."

"I don't know," Darcy said doubtfully. "Customers can be funny that way."

"Look, it's no different than if Caroline and Corbin had made it all the way through the ad series and then he hit her the night before the wedding."

"Except that you're planning the exit before the engagement ever gets off the ground. Of course, if you're going to be convincing to all your customers, you'll have to play it very close to your chest right up till the moment when you don't go through with the wedding. And that could be a problem."

"Interesting that you think so. Tell me why."

"Because if you're acting as if you're serious in public, the woman you choose as your supposed bride might get the idea that you really are. Serious, I mean—no matter what you tell her in private."

Trey nodded. "That's exactly what I was thinking. In fact, Dave pointed out that it could end up in something like a breach-of-promise case."

''He would say that. Skittish guys all think alike.''

He lifted an eyebrow at her. ''Skittish *guys?* You saw the problem just as quickly as Dave or I did.''

He'd caught her on that one. Darcy shrugged. ''So I guess that makes me a skittish girl.''

''And that's why...'' He raised his cup and sipped. The silence drew out.

Darcy felt her breath catch and wondered why she was feeling so anxious. All this had nothing to do with her. Or did it?

''That's why,'' Trey said very softly, ''Dave suggested that my supposed bride be...you.''

CHAPTER TWO

TREY hadn't spent a lot of time in his life contemplating proposals—how the question should be phrased, what the best occasion to ask it would be, or even who he might want to address it to. He figured there would be plenty of time to consider all that, because he was thirty-two and not in the least anxious to settle down.

But there was one thing he would never have expected—that when the day came and he actually suggested to a woman that the two of them might become engaged, she would choke on her coffee and turn purple at the very idea of becoming Mrs. Andrew Patrick Kent the Third.

Stunned and a bit dizzy, maybe—he could understand that sort of reaction. Shedding tears of joy, perhaps. Completely unable to speak and having to indicate agreement by gesturing, even.

But asphyxiating in shock?

Of course the notion of being Mrs. Kent wasn't what was actually sending Darcy Malone into coughing spasms at the moment. It couldn't be, because he'd made quite clear that an actual marriage wasn't what he was offering. She was gasping for air merely because he'd suggested she be his temporary fiancée.

And that made no sense whatsoever. Considering the number of women who'd angled for the position over the years, why was this one puffing in agony over the notion that she simply pretend for a while that she wanted the title?

"Darcy," he said. "If you could stop this for a minute and just listen…"

"If I *could* stop…" She clutched both hands to her

chest. Her voice was a barely understandable croak. "I *would*. Just go away, all right?"

"Not as long as you're threatening to strangle. Here, have a drink of water." He held a glass to her lips and she managed to sputter a few drops. Her coughs died down to a low wheeze, and he said, "There, that's better."

"Maybe it is from your point of view." She leaned weakly against the counter.

"Look, I don't understand what's so awful about the idea. I'm not asking you to have my baby, you know." He set the water glass down with a bump. "Most of the women I know would be flattered."

"Which is precisely why you're asking me, instead of one of them. Right?"

He nodded, relieved that she understood.

"Because I'm not fool enough to take you seriously. So there you have it."

Trey frowned. "I guess that didn't come out quite the way I intended it to."

"Maybe you'll figure out what I mean in a year or two. Or maybe I'll wake up in the middle of the night and see how that comment is really a compliment to me. But I wouldn't count on it."

"If you'd just listen to what I have in mind, I think you'd see it differently," he suggested. "There would be considerable advantages for you in this plan, you know."

"Name two."

"You need a job."

"I'll get one on my own, thanks. I'm perfectly well qualified."

Her tone was a bit truculent, just enough to make him suspicious. Trey wished he'd thought to ask Dave exactly why she was unemployed at the moment.

"I could make it easy for you," he said. "You said you're applying to the Kentwells chain—"

"And what do you think my working conditions would be like on any job you could give me? I'm sure my new supervisor would be simply delighted to have an employee foisted on him by the boss."

"I'm not stupid enough to make it obvious, Darcy."

"And exactly how are you going to keep it from being obvious? Are you planning to make the announcement about hiring me before or after my picture is splashed all over the newspapers and the airwaves, standing next to you and choosing lamps for our bedroom? Do you really think your other employees can't connect the dots and see what's going on?"

"All right, then—I'll get you a job somewhere else."

"I told you, I'll do it myself, on my own merits. I don't need a handout."

"Stubborn, aren't you? Dave said you were." Maybe that explained why she was here and not still wherever she'd been living. San Francisco—was that what Dave had told him?

"For a guy who's supposed to be devoted to the principles of confidentiality, Dave talks too much."

"You're not his client. I am."

"So he can talk to you about me, but he can't tell me about you? Oh, that's charming."

"Unless we're engaged. Then he can say pretty much whatever he wants because we'd be—in a sense—family."

"In a sense," she agreed. "You're not giving this idea up, are you?"

"I think it's the perfect arrangement."

"What makes it so great—if I'm allowed to ask?"

"For one thing, sudden engagements are always suspicious, but—"

Darcy's eyes widened. They were an odd shade of brownish-green, he noticed. Trey had never seen anything quite like them.

"What?" she gasped. "You're saying you don't believe in love at first sight?"

He ignored the irony dripping from her voice. "But since you're my friend's sister and not just some stranger, we could easily have met months or even years ago. You've lived out of town for a while, so that explains why my other friends haven't met you or heard about you. But since I travel a fair amount, I could have been visiting you often. They'll believe it."

"*Not just some stranger...* That sounds like a great title for a made-for-TV movie."

She said it under her breath, but there was no missing the fact that Darcy had gone past irony all the way into sarcasm, so Trey pretended he hadn't heard her. "People will still be startled when I announce that I'm getting married, of course—"

"I don't doubt that a bit."

"But not as startled as they would be if I said I was engaged to someone they'd known all along."

She nodded. "Someone you've obviously not been serious about before."

He was making progress, Trey told himself. He could almost see the dents starting to show in her armor. "Right. You're the unknown, so they'll reserve judgment for a while. And it's conceivable that I could have fallen in love with you, so—"

She rubbed her temple as if it hurt. "Gee, thanks. I feel so honored."

Trey felt like swearing. What on earth had he said that was so terrible? She was easy on the eyes, she had a graceful walk, she projected a certain confidence even in ragged sweat clothes. If he could just surgically remove that sharp tongue, she'd be next door to perfect for the role. "I was paying you a compliment."

"Drop it, Trey. You're only digging yourself a deeper hole, here."

"Anyway, the fact that we're admitting we've only seen each other at random intervals will even help account for why the whole thing falls apart in the end—when we break off the engagement."

"Because when we start spending lots of time together, we'll realize we aren't as compatible as we thought we were."

"Exactly."

"Well, that's not hard for me to picture," she said. "You really have thought of everything."

"It's not like this will last forever, Darcy."

"But it will go on for a while." She sighed. "Just for the sake of discussion, and not because I'm agreeing to anything, how long do you expect it would take?"

Trey stopped to calculate. "Two or three weeks."

"How did you come up with that? I thought you said it was going to be a three-month long campaign."

"Well, yes—we've bought ad space that far ahead. I mean it'll be two or—more likely—three weeks for photography and production. We'll have to start from scratch, you see."

"And after the shooting's done, everything just runs on autopilot?"

He frowned. "I suppose there would be the occasional public appearance, just to keep up the fiction, until the ads finished running."

"That's what I thought. Somewhere around Christmastime, in other words."

"It's not like it would be every day. Dave said there's no one in your life, so—"

"And since I obviously don't have anything better to do for the next few months, I might as well do this?"

"That isn't quite the way I'd have put it, but…"

"Pardon me while I go ask my brother to refer me to a good attorney."

Trey wrinkled his brow. "Dave *is* an attorney, Darcy."

"Yes. But after I murder him, I'm going to need someone else to defend me."

"Dave has only your best interests at heart. You're at loose ends right now, and a job hunt may take months, especially since you're not working at the moment. Employers always want to know what happened to the last job."

She sighed as if she'd found that out the hard way.

Trey pushed his advantage. "I'm willing to compensate you for the time you spend with me."

"Oh, thanks very much for making me sound like a call girl."

"It's nothing of the sort! You'd have a paying job right away, even if it's not exactly what you've been applying for. And within a few weeks, by the time the photography's all finished, I'm sure I can arrange something for you that's closer to your field."

"Any job you could possibly arrange for me would look very fishy."

She had a point, and Trey had to admit it. "All right, if an easy-to-get job isn't your thing, then what sort of bargain do you have in mind? There must be something you want."

"You mean, if I could have anything at all?"

He noted a sudden gleam in her eyes. Greed, he thought. Or avarice. Or maybe just plain ambition. "Within reason," he said warily.

"Then I want my own firm."

He was waiting for her to say *a million dollars,* and so it took a few seconds for him to register what she'd actually demanded. "I said within reason, Darcy."

"I think I'm being perfectly reasonable. I don't want you

to set me up with a Fortune-500-sized company. I just want my own, one-person graphic-design firm.''

''And you think it wouldn't look suspicious if I was behind that?''

''Who's going to know you're behind it? I'm tired of working for other people. I'm tired of producing infinite variations of dull subjects. I want to be able to choose which projects I handle, and set my own work schedule.''

''Being in business for yourself isn't all it's cracked up to be.''

''It's better than having to deal with a boss who's been stuck with me against his will. You help me set up my office. Then after we break our engagement, the Kentwells chain hires me to create a new logo and—''

''Wait a minute here.''

''That will prove to everyone that we're breaking up amicably, remaining friends despite the fact that the wedding didn't work out. Then you can recommend me to the other firms you deal with, and we'll be square.''

''That's outrageous. In fact, it's blackmail.''

''It's business. Take it or leave it.''

''And if I leave it?''

Darcy shrugged. ''That would be just fine with me. I'll be no worse off than when I woke up this morning—except for the attack of acid indigestion you've caused me. And I'm sure you could find someone among the women of your acquaintance who would play along with the idea of being engaged and be much more enthusiastic about the role than I am.''

She had him there. They'd be too enthusiastic—that was the problem.

''One of Caroline's friends might be willing to help you out.''

Trey couldn't help wincing at the thought.

''And if Dave put his mind to it,'' she went on thoughtfully, "he might even be able to write up a contract that's watertight enough to keep her from suing you later on for changing your mind and dumping her. Mind you, I'm not promising anything of the sort, because then I'd be practicing law without a license, and Dave says I have to be very careful about that."

Might. Trey didn't feel like betting his life on Dave's contract-writing skills. Which of course was exactly why Darcy had said it. Obviously Dave wasn't the only member of the Malone family who specialized in twisted legal logic.

"If I agree to set you up in business," he warned, "I'm going to expect a lot more than the occasional public appearance."

Darcy didn't miss a beat. "Really? What have you got in mind? You want me to have your baby after all?"

His mouth went dry at the thought. *With horror,* he told himself. "Heaven forbid the world should have a miniature version of you inflicted on it."

Darcy smiled. "Now that's really funny, because I was thinking precisely the same thing about you. Andrew Patrick Kent the Fourth—the poor child. What would you call him, anyway? Quatro?"

Trey decided to ignore her. "If I'm going to invest serious money in setting you up in business, you'd have to make yourself available whenever I needed you. And there would be no embarrassing incidents. No getting caught in a compromising position with some other guy."

"Oh, that's comforting. You mean I can do anything I want, as long as I don't get caught—right?"

"Dammit, Darcy—"

"Oh, don't worry. Remember? I'm just as skittish as you are—there's absolutely no one in my life and no possibility that will change. So you have nothing to worry about. I'll be too busy working on my new business to look around for men, anyway."

He wished that felt like a benefit. In fact, the more she worked on her new business, he suspected, the more this was going to cost him. But what choice did he have? "Then we have a deal," he said, and held out a hand.

She hesitated, and he found himself holding his breath. Then she reached out. Her palm was warm against his, her grip firm, her fingers steady.

Trey wouldn't have been surprised to find that he was trembling himself. Which was totally ridiculous, of course. She'd agreed to the terms—hell, she'd set them herself, so she had nothing to complain about. Things were perfectly clear. It was absolutely, unquestionably a no-risk agreement.

So why did he feel like running?

Darcy had had no intention of agreeing. The proposition Trey had made was nothing short of ludicrous, but the only way to make him realize how silly he sounded had seemed to be to make her terms just as laughable as his were. So she'd fired back in similar terms, never dreaming that he might actually give in and accept them.

For a moment, when he'd offered to shake hands on the deal, she'd been tempted to back down—to withdraw the demand of a business of her own and take him up on the offer to help her find a job instead.

But all the arguments she'd given him earlier were valid ones. If he were to create a job for her, she'd go into it under a cloud. Though her skills and talents were real, a supervisor who was forced to hire her might never give her the chance to make good. If that were to happen, the working conditions could end up being every bit as bad as what she'd left behind when she came home to the penthouse.

And once Trey had found her a job, he would have fulfilled his end of the bargain, and he'd have no further obligation to help, no matter how unpleasant the situation in which she found herself. Meanwhile, she'd still have her promise to fulfill, even if it took months and months...

But what was she thinking? There was yet another option—a third choice, beyond making a deal for either a job or her own business. And the third alternative was the only sensible one. She should thank him for his offer and do her best not to laugh as she turned him down.

But she didn't. Instead, as if she were mesmerized, Darcy found herself reaching out to him, actually agreeing to be his pretend fiancée for the next three months.

What in heaven's name was wrong with her? She should have run, not let herself be talked into cutting a deal with Mr. Elegance. He was exactly what she didn't need—another guy who was gorgeous and knew how to use it to his advantage...

No, she thought. This time would be different. This time, she was the one who would be doing the using.

She vaguely heard the creak of Dave's office door opening, and only when she heard the murmur of approaching voices did she realize that she and Trey were still standing in the kitchen, hand in hand. She pulled away as quickly as she could.

But obviously Dave had already seen, for he said, "You've struck a deal, then? Good—I'll get the paperwork written up."

"Paperwork?" Darcy said. "You mean like a prenuptial agreement?"

Trey frowned at her.

"All right, a nonnuptial agreement, then," Darcy muttered.

Dave had gone straight on. "I'll draw up a simple contract. I'm glad we could help out, Trey."

"What do you mean, *we?*" Darcy said. "Unless you're going to be getting your picture taken, Dave, and making nice at social functions, I don't think that your contribution is nearly as personal as—''

Caroline spoke up. ''Speaking of social functions, will you be giving Darcy an engagement party, David?''

''It hadn't crossed my mind, no.''

Darcy relaxed. At least Dave hadn't totally lost his perspective.

Caroline frowned. ''Then perhaps I'll do it. I don't think it matters who hosts it, really—does it, Darcy? I know showers are supposed to be given by friends, not by family members, but is there any rule about engagement parties?''

Was the woman serious? Hadn't she gotten the message that this wasn't real? Or was Trey planning to keep her in the dark, too?

Darcy decided to humor her for a bit and wait for Trey to speak up or Caroline to regain her senses. ''Beats me. As long as we're shopping for everything a couple needs for a wedding and a home, maybe we should start with an etiquette book so we can look up the rules.''

Caroline smiled, and then touched a careful finger to her upper lip where the skin had stretched wide and broken open once again. ''Ouch, that hurt. But that's a really good idea. Every bride should have an etiquette book on hand. I think this is going to be wonderful, Trey—Darcy has much more creative ideas than I do.''

''Yes,'' Trey said, almost under his breath. ''I'd already noticed how creative she is at getting what she wants.''

''I'll start planning the party, then,'' Caroline went on. ''Surely by the weekend I'll be able to appear in public, don't you think? I'm a fast healer.''

Fast healer? Darcy wondered if that meant Caroline had experience in how long it took her to heal from facial blows, and suddenly she felt a little selfish at having thought only of the impact this agreement would have on her own life. If by playing this part for a while she could make Caroline's life a little easier, spare her some embarrassment over her broken engagement, and help her pick up the pieces of a shattered dream so that she didn't become involved with yet another abusive man somewhere down the line...

Now that's a great motive, she told herself. *It sounds so much nicer of me than simply blackmailing Trey Kent into setting me up in business...*

Her head was obviously still spinning. How had she gotten herself so enmeshed in this? And *why?* That was the real puzzler. Certainly not to help Caroline, whom she didn't even know, or Trey, whom she didn't even like!

"This is wonderful," Caroline bubbled. "It's all working out better than anyone could have hoped. Just a couple of hours ago I thought I'd ruined everything, but now it's going to be even better than I thought was possible."

Trey was looking at his watch. "Caroline, about the district attorney—what have you decided to do?"

Caroline's glee vanished. She took a deep breath. "I'll talk to him. And I'll file charges."

"Good." Trey squeezed her shoulder. "I'll be right there with you all the way."

There was a soft note in his voice that was unlike anything Darcy had heard before. She was still trying to sort out whether it was approval, support, warmth, love, or something else entirely, when he turned to her.

"Darcy, I'll pick you up at six, and we can spend the evening going over the necessary details so you'll be prepared for the shoot tomorrow." Every hint of softness was gone.

"How considerate of you to ask whether that fits into my calendar," she murmured, making no attempt to keep the sarcasm out of her tone. "And here I expected maybe you'd be dictatorial about your plans."

"I suppose we could go in without any preparation and

just let the crew think we were too busy making love to bother to talk,'' Trey said.

Darcy noticed her brother biting back a grin, and glared at him. ''Six will be fine.''

''I thought it would,'' Trey murmured.

Irritated, Darcy struck back. ''Now you must run along and get busy, darling,'' she said sweetly, ''because you'll need to make all the money you possibly can, in order to provide for me.''

When Trey arrived at the cottage on the dot of six o'clock, Darcy was still struggling to make the computer print out a will she'd been working on most of the afternoon. ''Have a seat while I finish,'' she told him. ''Dave needs this first thing in the morning.''

He sat on the corner of the desk, right next to her, rather than in the chair she indicated. ''Word processing isn't exactly your top skill?''

''If you're trying to make the point that I'd be happier doing graphic arts instead of wills, don't bother. We all know that already.'' She pushed a key and the printer wheezed, sucked in a sheet of paper and stopped dead.

''What's the rush with the will?'' Trey said.

''Since it's not your will, that information is confidential.'' Darcy tried the print command again, but the printer refused to budge. ''Okay, I get the message. Maybe it just needs to pout for a while. I want to be home early anyway because it's been a very long day. So I'll come back and finish this up later.'' She closed the file and turned off the computer. ''Let's go.''

''Aren't you going to change clothes?''

Darcy glanced at her slacks and sweater. ''Why? Where are we going? Because if you're planning to take me someplace swanky, I'd suggest you think again.''

''There will be some formal events along the way, you

know," Trey warned. "If you're not comfortable with that, we've got a problem."

"Oh, I can handle swank—as long as you provide the clothes. I just meant that you surely don't want to talk about all this at one of your regular hangouts and risk being overheard by your friends."

"Good point. Where do you suggest?"

She looked him over thoughtfully. "There's a little bar a few blocks down. It's noisy enough that nobody can be overheard, and dark enough not to be noticed—that is, if you lose the tie and borrow one of Dave's windbreakers to replace the suit coat. Try the back of his office door."

When he came back, he was shrugging himself into an oversized black jacket emblazoned in huge yellow letters with the name of the college where Dave had gotten his law degree. "This isn't exactly what I'd call anonymous. I bet it glows in the dark."

"It'll fit into the crowd at Tanner's better than that suit would."

"You're sure Dave won't mind me borrowing it? Where is he, anyway?"

"I don't know. He left an hour or so ago and said something vague about having an appointment."

He helped her into her raincoat. Darcy checked her pockets for keys and emergency funds and locked the door of the cottage behind them.

His car was parked directly in front. It was—of course—a fire-engine-red sports car that Darcy's gut said had cost at least twice as much as her entire college education. *Men are so predictable...* "Oh, boy," she said. "How many miles does this baby get per gallon of testosterone?"

"I have no idea," Trey said coolly. "It belongs to Caroline."

"All right," she admitted cheerfully. "I leaped to conclusions there and missed the pier entirely. So what do you drive—a Rolls-Royce that matches your suit?"

"Depends on the day."

Darcy had to admit that despite herself she was impressed—certainly not by the fact that he owned multiple cars, but because he didn't seem to want to brag about it. "How did you and Dave become friends, anyway? Somehow the two of you just don't seem the type to be bosom buddies."

"Because he has a motorcycle and I don't?"

Darcy chalked that up as a fact to remember. "I've never heard him mention your name."

"We met in the frat house in college. Lost track of each other after that, and we didn't run into each other again until a college reunion a year or two ago."

"When I'd already gone to San Francisco."

"I guess it must have been. What were you doing out there, anyway?"

"Graphic arts," she said crisply. "How long have you been with the stores?"

"About two years. I stayed out East after grad school and worked for a couple of different firms, but then my dad had a heart attack and had to retire, so I came home to take over."

"How does he feel about you being in charge?"

"He died six months ago," Trey said.

"I'm sorry. I didn't know."

"No reason you should."

That, Darcy thought, was not quite true, even though the name probably wouldn't have had personal meaning for her. But six months ago she'd been living in a fog where nothing much had made an impression. Six months ago, she might not even have noticed Trey Kent if he'd crossed her path.

No, she thought. No matter what else was going on in

her life, it would be impossible for any woman to ignore Mr. Elegance.

"Where are we going, again?"

Darcy had gotten so sidetracked into thinking about Trey that she had to stop to think. "Tanner's—it's a couple more blocks down. There's parking out front." Belatedly she remembered what he was driving. "Unless you'd rather leave the car with a valet at the hotel down the street."

"No, it'll be fine. This car has such an elaborate alarm system it'll slap handcuffs on anybody who tries to touch it, long before the cops have a chance to show up."

Just inside the front door of the bar, she paused to look around. "There's a free booth—I'll grab it, if you want to go get the drinks. Just an iced tea for me, please."

The booth was in a corner, well away from both the door and the bar, and she had to work her way through a fair-sized crowd to get there. Halfway there, she heard someone calling her name and turned to see a friend of Dave's leaning against the pool table.

"What brings you back to town, Darcy?" he asked. "Dave isn't sick or something, is he?"

"He's fine, Joe."

"Well, I haven't seen him around much. And last I heard you were hanging out in San Francisco with Pete Willis."

Darcy kept her voice even, but it took an effort. "That's old news, I'm afraid."

"You and Pete called it quits? Well, let me buy you a beer and you can bring me up-to-date. Must be a year since I've seen you."

Behind him, Trey said levelly, "She's drinking iced tea, and she's with me tonight."

Joe cocked his chin forward. "I don't see any ownership tag hanging around her neck. No ring on her finger."

"Check again tomorrow and you might be surprised," Trey said. He stepped between them.

"Later, Joe," Darcy called. She took her iced tea and considered dumping it over Trey's head. Which was surely an odd reaction, considering that she was relieved to have Joe's interrogation short-circuited. Still, just because Joe asked questions didn't mean she intended to answer them, and it wasn't up to Trey to decide who she talked to. "You want to tell me what that was all about—besides disgustingly primitive primate behavior?"

"He was hassling you."

"He was asking how I was."

"Who's Pete Willis?"

"Oh, is that what's bothering you? He's the man I worked with in San Francisco. Nobody you need to be worried about."

"He's not going to be coming around wanting to hire you back?"

"Not in this lifetime." Her voice was steady. "Let's get our business taken care of before Joe has another beer and decides to find out whether you can whip him."

Trey seemed only mildly interested. "Who are you worried about coming out the worse for wear—him or me?"

"Neither. I don't want Dave to have to come bail everybody out of jail, because I'll end up doing the paperwork. Tell me about the ad campaign."

Trey leaned back against the vinyl seat. "Since we'd already started with Caroline and Corbin, the ad department is having to revamp the entire shooting schedule."

"Corbin. What a name."

"It fits him. The idea is to minimize setup time for each photo by working through the store in a logical way, not necessarily in the same order the ads will appear. We'll do the engagement ring tomorrow, of course, because that's the first ad which will run and they need the art right away. But then we may do household linens and lawn furniture, because they're in the same section of the store. You know how the departments are laid out in sort of a rough circle.''

"Actually," Darcy said, "no, I don't. I haven't been in a Kentwells store in years."

Trey blinked in surprise. "Oh, of course. All our stores are in Chicago, and you've been out west."

She said, very slowly, "Yes." It was true, as far as it went. And there was no point in alienating him by telling the whole truth—that she'd always preferred to do her shopping with Kentwells's competition. *You wouldn't volunteer that information if you were interviewing for a job,* she reminded herself. *This isn't much different.*

"We'll have to start early in the morning," he warned. "There's still a lot of prep work to be done because we're starting from scratch with you."

Starting from scratch... "You'd better smile when you say that, partner. I'm not exactly in the frame of mind to play Cinderella."

Trey sighed. "I do keep putting my foot in my mouth, don't I? I just meant that the clothes which were chosen for Caroline won't work for you, and the hairstyle and makeup you need will be much different, too."

A woman in a white jacket deposited a pizza on the table between them and went away without a word. Trey looked at it in puzzlement. "Did we order this?"

"Sort of. It's my standing order—I just wave at Jessie in the kitchen whenever I come in." She took a paper plate from the stack on the table and slid a steaming wedge onto it. "Try it, it's the best hand-thrown pizza in town. Since you brought up Caroline, I had a question. She does understand this is all made up, right?"

"Of course."

"Because she seems to be a bit of a dreamer. She's not serious about the engagement party, is she?"

"Of course she is. The best way to make it convincing

is for everyone around us to act as if it's real. Caroline throwing a party, Dave giving a toast to the happy couple— it all adds a touch of reality.'' He helped himself to a slice of pizza. ''Now—let's get down to business. Tell me everything I could possibly need to know about my wife-to-be.''

CHAPTER THREE

No SOONER had his request popped out than Trey regretted it—or at least he regretted the way he had phrased it. Asking a woman to tell him all about herself—what had he been thinking?

He'd never met one yet who wouldn't take that as a blanket invitation to share an entire evening's worth of self-analysis. By the time Darcy finished her Freud act, he'd probably known what she'd had for breakfast on her first day of school, and all about the lasting wounds it had left on her psyche.

Why hadn't he settled for asking simple, straightforward questions that would elicit the facts he needed without including hours worth of padding—explanations that would make it practically impossible to keep his eyes open?

"Age twenty-seven," Darcy said crisply. "Born and raised in the west suburbs of Chicago, parents died eight years ago in a car accident. I finished my degree, worked at a PR firm downtown, then spent some time in San Francisco, and came back here. Anything else?" She tore another slice of pizza from the pie and took a big bite, obviously finished talking for the moment.

Trey was too stunned at the machine-gun approach to comment.

She obviously took his continued silence for a lack of further questions, because she swallowed and said, "If I'd realized that's all you wanted to know, I'd have given you one of my job applications this morning and saved you the trouble of asking. Are you all right?"

"I was just thinking that if I'd asked Caroline how she

felt, I'd still be sitting here listening in a couple of hours. Ask you for a rundown of your life and you're finished in fifteen seconds.''

Darcy shrugged. ''Mine hasn't been a terribly exciting life.''

''Normally for a female that's no bar to talking about it at length,'' Trey said dryly.

''Oh, so that must be why you're not interested in actually getting married—because women are boring and self-centered and don't know when to shut up.''

He knew better than to think there was a safe answer to that. ''I've known a few talkative types,'' he admitted. ''But the fact is I'm not established well enough to even think about marriage just now.'' She'd never believe that he was telling the truth, but at least it might distract her.

Darcy rolled her eyes. ''Right. A hundred-year-old department store chain isn't stable enough to support a wife... And I trusted you to set me up in business? I knew I needed my head examined.''

''You made an agreement,'' Trey pointed out.

''And I'll hold you to your end of the bargain. In the meantime, however, I suppose there are some things we should work out before we go public with this act.''

''Like what?''

''Like when we supposedly met. How long we've supposedly been dating. When we're supposedly getting married.''

''Maybe we could agree to leave the *supposedly* out of this and act as if it's real.''

She shrugged. ''If you like. I thought perhaps you'd feel more comfortable if I was continually reminding myself that it *wasn't* real. But you're the boss. Which reminds me—you said the photo crew had already started working with Caroline and Corbin as the models. How are you going to explain the sudden change?''

"Corbin's been called out of town on business."

"Really?"

"No, but I expect he'll decide to make himself scarce until I've cooled off enough not to kill him."

Darcy sat back in the booth seat and looked him over thoughtfully, her lips pursed.

"What?" Trey asked.

"I was just noticing this violent streak in you. First you threaten Joe, who might be a nuisance but is certainly nothing more. And even though Corbin sounds like the worst kind of bad guy—"

"I didn't threaten your pal Joe. You're the one who suggested if he had another beer he'd be threatening me. I was merely commenting that I'm perfectly able to take care of myself if he does. And where Corbin is concerned, I was talking about what he's thinking just now—that if he lies low for a while, it'll all blow over. Personally, I'd much rather send him to jail, and then ruin him when he finally comes out, than to actually end his miserable existence."

"Oh, *that's* comforting."

"Good," Trey said. "Glad we got that settled. So after your parents died, it was just you and Dave? No wonder he pulled the parent act, telling you to be careful who you dated. And that must be why he never talked about having a little sister, either. He felt responsible for you."

Darcy smiled. "Or else he didn't trust his frat brothers. I wouldn't know which it was. But that's all ancient history. When are we supposedly…"

He wagged a finger at her.

"Oh, all right. When are we getting married?"

A cold trickle edged down Trey's spine. It made him sit up just a little straighter.

"What's the matter?"

Trey shook his head a little and smiled. "Nothing. Just for an instant there, I had the same sensation I felt one night right before I realized I was being stalked by a mugger.''

"Thanks very much. I love being bracketed with muggers.''

"Don't take it personally. It's just a tingle—a sense of danger lurking. My grandmother used to say someone was walking over her grave.''

"Now there's a cozy thought for you. What happened with the mugger?''

"Well, I didn't marry him,'' Trey said calmly.

"So we can assume it's not quite the same feeling after all? Good. You were going to tell me when the wedding's going to be.''

"Since I don't plan to put the event on my calendar, I don't see why we have to set an actual date.''

"You *are* a skittish one, aren't you? Because people will ask when the wedding is, that's why—and if you don't have an answer, they'll think it's odd. And then they'll expect to be invited—when it comes up to the time when the invitations should go out, they'll be hurt if they don't receive one. It won't occur to them to think that no one else has been invited, either.''

"I hadn't thought about it quite that way.''

"Well, of course you hadn't. Since you're planning to wrap up this ad campaign right at Christmas, let's set the date for Christmas Eve.''

Trey frowned. "Wouldn't that look suspicious? I mean, right on the holiday?''

"It's a great excuse for keeping the whole thing small. We can say that we're inviting just a few people and having the ceremony at a time when the few relatives I have will be home for the holidays.''

"Will they be? Your relatives, I mean—home for the holidays.''

"Probably not, but it's still a good explanation for why we're not sending hundreds of invitations."

Trey shook his head. "I don't know. Society's apt to ask what we're hiding—especially after the big splash all the way through the engagement."

"After sharing all of that with the public, we'll tell them we deserve a little privacy. Besides, the fewer invitations you actually send, the fewer people you'll have to notify when you call it off at the last minute. Why invite the world and then have to phone them all to cancel? Why draw attention to the fact that you're not carrying through with your plans?"

"We could just set the date for sometime next year, and not bother with invitations at all."

"And exactly what would be the point of the ad campaign if it just trickles off with a vague promise of a wedding to be held some indefinite time in the distant future?"

Trey rubbed his jaw. "You're saying the campaign needs a climactic moment, so to speak."

"All ad campaigns do. At the least, you don't want it to have an anticlimactic moment."

"All right, you've convinced me. Christmas Eve it is. I suppose that does make everything easier. Holly and red velvet for the bridesmaids—"

"That would be such a cliché," Darcy said. "Every woman in the city would see that one coming. I hope your ad department people are more creative than you are."

"Thanks," Trey said.

"But then they must be," Darcy said kindly, "because they've kept the stores in business for a hundred years. Right? How many stores do you have?"

But she didn't seem to be listening for an answer. She looked past him just as he opened his mouth to reply, and he watched her eyes widen. The sense of danger trickled down his spine again. It was odd that he hadn't thought of his grandmother's old saying in years, only to find himself contemplating it twice within a few minutes. So what was it this time?

"What's up?" he asked. "Has your pal Joe finally consumed enough liquid courage to challenge me?"

"He's not my pal, he's Dave's."

Trey looked over his shoulder. Three paces from the table, Joe stopped almost in midstep. For a moment an internal war showed on his face, and then he turned on his heel and shuffled away.

"Very impressive," Darcy said. "Cowing him like that without uttering a word."

"Oh, you should see them run when I'm wearing a tie." He kept his voice dry. "If I actually pull the knot loose to get ready for action, you can hardly get out of their way, they scamper so fast."

She nodded. "You should have told me that making you give up your necktie was about the same as taking a cop's gun away from him. Look, I've pretty much lost my appetite, and as long as we've got the important things settled—"

"You'd like to get back to that will you were struggling with."

She sighed. "Something like that."

At the door of the cottage, he held out a hand for her key, but Darcy ignored him and unlocked the door herself. "I'll meet you at the store in the morning, then," she said.

It was so plainly a dismissal that Trey had to smile. What did she expect, that he'd try to force his way in and stay the night just so he just could take her to work with him the next morning?

He wondered idly whether seducing her would be worth the trouble. Probably not, he decided. This woman was dangerous enough without taking her to bed and giving her all sorts of new ideas.

"I do need to come inside to get my tie and return Dave's jacket," he pointed out smoothly.

"Oh. Of course." She didn't seem eager to stand aside to allow him in, but she wasn't in a hurry to turn the lights on, either. If she had been any other woman, he would have interpreted that as a hint, because kisses stolen in the dark seemed to be so much more romantic to the female of the species. But then Darcy didn't fit the mold in a lot of ways.

He considered kissing her good-night just to prove he could, and concluded that she was likely to haul off and slug him. In that case, by morning he and Caroline would be a matched set, and the ad campaign would be right back in the soup. No, stealing a kiss would make no sense whatsoever.

And he should have himself committed for even thinking about doing anything more than that—though the simple truth didn't do much to stop him from considering all the possibilities.

He quietly got his suit coat from where he'd left it in Dave's office, draped his tie around his neck once more and paused at the door. "You'll be all right here alone?"

"I live here," she pointed out.

He looked around. "Yeah, Dave said something about that. Where?"

"There's a sort of apartment upstairs."

"Sort of?"

"Yes—why did you think I was taking a shower right next door to Dave's office?"

It hadn't occurred to him to think about it. "I guess I was a little preoccupied this morning."

"Of course you were. What time should I show up tomorrow?"

"I'll meet you in the restaurant of the mall store, nine o'clock. Is there actually a room upstairs? It looks like it couldn't be any more than an attic."

"Well, we call it the penthouse, but—"

He smiled. "So you really *are* Cinderella."

Darcy rolled her eyes. "In a manner of speaking. But don't worry about me getting swept away by the whole prince-and-the-palace thing. Not only are you *not* all that charming, but glass slippers would be pretty uncomfortable for everyday wear."

"Then it's just as well the store doesn't stock them," he said, and smiled.

Yes, he thought, Dave had been right—she was a marvelous choice. Sharp-witted, always on her toes, and not likely to forget for an instant the deal she'd made.

It was safe for him to relax.

The morning was dismal, with low-hanging gray clouds, a brisk wind, and a few drops of cold rain spattering against the cottage's dormer windows. Darcy rolled over, looked outside and seriously considered putting her head under the pillow and pretending that she'd never heard of Trey Kent.

Yesterday had all been a bad dream—hadn't it? From his incredibly arrogant statement that she should be flattered that he'd asked her to role-play in his little drama, all the way through the third-degree over pizza last night, she'd felt like she was caught in a surreal landscape where nothing was what it seemed.

Take that smile of his when he'd told her the Kentwells stores didn't carry glass slippers. It had been, she thought, the first real amusement she'd seen him show, and the effect on her had been like suddenly looking into a floodlight—she'd still been seeing spots when she'd climbed under the comforter on her futon and collapsed.

She sighed. Maybe if she just went back to sleep…

Then she remembered what a decided talent the man had for getting his own way, and she reluctantly dragged herself out of bed. She'd made an agreement, and she was stuck with it.

When Darcy came downstairs, Mrs. Cusack was already behind her desk, coughing and spluttering into a white linen handkerchief. She gave Darcy a very thin smile and a nasal good morning.

"I'm so glad you're feeling better," Darcy said. "I tried to leave everything in order for you. Except for Mrs. Johansson's will, I'm afraid. All the changes are made to it, but I couldn't get it to print."

The secretary sniffed.

Darcy wasn't sure whether that was a sinus symptom or a comment about the efficiency of her work. She decided it might be better not to find out for sure.

She spotted the stack of manila envelopes in the plastic tray at the corner of the desk and picked them up. There was no sense in mailing out job applications right now. Until she had a better feel for how long she'd be tied up shooting this ad campaign, she couldn't schedule interviews anyway. And until she had a better idea of whether she actually could manage to set up her own business—even with Trey Kent's help, it wasn't going to be a piece of cake—she'd better just put the whole job search on hold. "I'll put these upstairs out of your way, Mrs. C., and then I'll be—"

"Where are you taking those?" Mrs. Cusack demanded.

Darcy blinked in surprise. "These are my job applications. I figured you wouldn't want them occupying space on your desk."

"There are no job applications here."

Darcy looked more closely at the top envelope. Mrs. Cusack was right; though the envelopes had come from the same box Darcy had used when assembling her applications, the addresses were not the potential employers on Darcy's list, but some of Dave's clients. The secretary had obviously been very busy in the hour or so since she'd arrived at work.

"What happened to my applications?"

Mrs. Cusack snorted into her handkerchief again. "I can only guess, but if you ran them through the postage meter and left them stacked there in the outgoing mail tray, Mr. Malone no doubt dropped them off when he made his regular stop at the post office on his way home last night."

Darcy could feel a low, dull pounding starting at the back of her head. "That's just great," she muttered.

"If you didn't want them mailed," Mrs. Cusack said firmly, "then you should not have gotten them ready to go."

The woman truly had a gift for rubbing one's nose in the obvious, Darcy thought.

Now that she stopped to think about it, Darcy knew exactly what had happened. She'd been taken off guard by Trey's proposition yesterday, and then she'd been swamped in unfamiliar and unusually demanding work throughout the rest of the day. She hadn't given the applications another thought until right this minute.

She hadn't even noticed them missing—but she'd been in the kitchen last night when Dave had called to her that he was leaving. He could easily have scooped the mail up without her seeing him do it. And then a few minutes later Trey had come back and she'd been off balance for the rest of the evening…

Not that it mattered much, she supposed. Applying for jobs was such a hit-and-miss proposition that the dozen envelopes she'd sent out probably wouldn't bring a single phone call to request an interview. That was why she'd been planning to spend today getting another bunch of applications ready to go—because the more irons she kept in the fire, the more likely that one of them would get hot enough to make an impression. But now…

Trey had been right that it might be months before she found a position that was well-matched to her skills. And he'd also been correct that being unemployed at the moment didn't make things easier when it came to hunting for a job. Of course that situation hadn't exactly been her choice, but it was one of the reasons why the possibility of having her own firm was so exciting. She'd be a fool not to take advantage of every opportunity which presented itself.

Dave came through the front door, set his briefcase on top of Mrs. Cusack's desk, ignored the secretary's long-suffering sigh and reached for the stack of letters waiting for his signature.

"How was your appointment last night?" Darcy asked, and watched in fascination as the usually unflappable Dave turned slightly red. "Hey, do the bright pink ears mean that it actually wasn't an appointment, but a hot date?"

"Darcy…"

"Which reminds me, when am I going to actually meet Ginger? I'm really sorry, but I forgot to tell you yesterday that she called the night I was working on my applications. So if she's mad at me, I don't blame her a bit."

He looked at his wristwatch. "I thought you were going to get your picture taken today, Darcy."

"I am. I'm on my way. Why don't you invite Ginger over for dinner tonight?"

"I suppose you're offering to cook."

"Sure. I can warm up takeout Chinese with the best of them."

Dave pulled out his fountain pen. "Is that what you're going to wear for your big debut? Jeans and a sweater?"

"Hey, big brother, you don't think Trey Kent's intended bride would be caught dead wearing anything that's hanging in *my* closet, do you?"

He made a noise that might have been agreement, and

then frowned. "There's actually a closet up in the penthouse? Funny—I never knew that."

"Bride?" Mrs. Cusack said at the same moment. "Who's the bride?"

Darcy wrinkled her nose. How had she managed to forget that Mrs. Cusack was right there, listening closely?

"Dave will tell you all about it," she said sweetly. "Now I must run, or I'll be late."

Since she was a few minutes early, Darcy drove all the way around the enormous parking lot at the mall. At the Kentwells end, the biggest mall in the state was just starting to come to life for the day, with a scattering of cars and a few people coming and going. Employees and mall-walkers, most likely.

At the far end of the mall, however, traffic was brisk. The Tyler-Royale department store must be having a sale, she thought, for there was a sizable cluster of people waiting outside the doors.

Too bad I can't check it out. Not that she had any extra money to spend right at the moment, even if she could use some new clothes that were suitable for job interviews or working in Dave's office.

She parked her car near the Kentwells store and walked across the lot to what looked like the main door. Since it had literally been years since she'd been inside, she wasn't sure exactly where the store's restaurant was located, but she was pleased to see it was not far from the entrance, halfway between the cosmetics counters near the door she'd come in and the big archway that led toward the other mall stores.

It was more like a snack bar than a restaurant, though, filled with small round tables and metal chairs of the sort found in old-fashioned ice-cream parlors. The lights were dim and the place seemed to be deserted, though rattling noises from a doorway behind the service bar indicated that it would soon come to life. She hoped it didn't take long, because she could use a cup of coffee to fire her up for the morning's work—whatever that turned out to be. The way Trey had described it, the most challenging assignment was likely going to be standing still and holding a pose, looking interested in a porch swing or a turkey roaster.

But then Trey had referred to this little snack area as a restaurant. Plainly they didn't see everything through the same color glasses.

She glanced at her watch and took a chair near the low wall which separated the restaurant from women's clothing. Good—she'd be sitting here waiting for Trey when he showed up at nine o'clock. Being early couldn't hurt her image. And after the impression she'd made yesterday, running around with her hair in a towel at the start of the business day, he'd probably be amazed.

A quarter of an hour later, she was still sitting there, doodling on a paper napkin and beginning to feel puzzled. It wasn't like him to be late.

She caught herself up short and laughed at the presumption which had come so naturally to her mind. *It isn't like him to be late…*

What was she thinking? She had no idea what the man's habits were. He'd shown up at the cottage last night at the precise moment when he'd told her he'd be there—but being on time once was hardly a guarantee that he made a habit of it.

The fact that he was Dave's friend was certainly no assurance that the man didn't have faults. Not only did Dave have a few flaws of his own—actually, more than just a few, if she was honest—but the things he considered to be deal-breakers in a friendship probably weren't the same ones Darcy would react strongly over.

Dave's friend Joe, the one she'd run into in the bar last

night, was all the proof she needed of that. He *was* capable of picking a fight—and Trey had obviously been just as capable of taking him on. It was interesting, though, how Joe had met Trey's gaze and almost stumbled over himself to get away....

At any rate, Joe was a nice enough guy. Of course, Dave had never set her up to date him. Dave was far was more careful of her than that.

But then, it wasn't like she was really engaged to Trey, either. So the fact that Dave had been involved in creating this mess didn't mean Trey was any more suitable than Joe was.

Probably far from it, if her own radar system was to be trusted. Take that smile of his...

As if a charming smile, capable of lighting up a room, would be enough to disarm her. Never again would she take things at face value—not after her experience with Pete Willis. Still, it would be prudent to exercise caution around Trey. In the charm department, Pete looked like a bumbling amateur next to Trey.

"And don't make any assumptions," she told herself.

An instant too late, she heard footsteps approaching, and sat up straighter.

"Talk to yourself a lot, do you?" Trey asked.

"Only when I've been sitting around and waiting for twenty minutes."

"That's why I came looking for you. We were supposed to meet in the restaurant, and you didn't show up."

Darcy frowned and waved a hand. "This looks like a restaurant to me."

Trey pulled a walkie-talkie out of his pocket. "Found her, Jason." The radio crackled unintelligibly and he put it back. "Well, now that you mention it, I guess I shouldn't have been surprised at the mixup. After that extraordinary eating place you took me to last night—"

"You're saying this isn't a restaurant? Chairs, tables, napkins, what looks like a soda fountain—"

"It isn't The Restaurant." His tone made the capital letters apparent. "This is the coffee bar—quick snacks and drinks only. Come on upstairs—everybody's waiting."

Great start, Darcy. You're really getting off on the right foot. So much for making an impression on him...

"What are you doing, anyway?"

She folded the napkin she'd been doodling on. "Experimenting with a logo for my new business." She thought she saw him give a tiny shudder at the reminder, which made her feel a bit better. "What was wrong with Tanner's, anyway? You said you liked the pizza."

Trey didn't answer, just led the way up the escalator and across the top floor of the store to a corner where he pulled open a wide, obviously heavy, mirrored door. Beyond the door was a big room paneled with dark walnut and more mirrors, separated into sections by polished wood columns and filled with furniture that looked both comfortable and antique. In the center of the room, tables draped with snowy white cloths had been pushed aside to make room for several racks of clothes. Yet another table had been cleared to hold a makeup station and a cushy-looking chair had been pulled up alongside.

As if someone had called them to attention, every person in the room went silent and turned to look at them.

"I see what you mean about a restaurant," Darcy said. "The one downstairs doesn't hold a candle to this. I don't suppose the kitchen would be able to whip up a cappuccino?"

A man who had been standing near the makeup station, bushy black eyebrows drawn together and arms folded across his chest, said, "Not till it opens at twelve o'clock. Let's get started. We're behind schedule as it is."

"Jason," Trey said. "Surely someone around here is

qualified to run the cappuccino maker. Darcy's doing us a favor—we can at least get her a cup of coffee. Honey, Jason's the store's advertising manager.''

Jason—that was the one Trey had radioed to say that he'd found her. Darcy looked at the man with interest, as much because of Trey's tone of voice as the introduction. He'd sounded almost conciliatory.

"Never mind," she said. "I can do without the caffeine. I'm just surprised that you've turned the restaurant into a dressing room.''

A white-haired woman who'd been straightening clothes on a rack turned to face her. "We obviously will need more room than for the average tryout."

That was true enough. Even a single one of the racks wouldn't have fit into an ordinary dressing room, in Darcy's estimation, and there were four racks in all. Each was crammed with clothes, and an overflow supply was laid out on tables nearby.

"Darcy, Arabella is the head of the women's clothing department," Trey said. "And Justine is the manager of the cosmetics section. I'll let you get down to work, ladies. Phone my office when you're ready for me."

Darcy took a step forward. "You're not going to stay?"

Trey gave her his million-watt smile.

Darcy felt her stomach flutter. *Remember,* she told herself. *No assumptions. He's performing for the crowd, not for you.*

"I'm flattered that you'd feel more secure if I stayed here, but I do have a chain of stores to run."

"Secure, nothing," Darcy said. "You mean nobody's going to be doing you over from head to toe? You're just going to show up for photos in that suit?"

"I hope you're not suggesting there's something wrong with my suit."

As a matter of fact, Darcy had to admit, there wasn't.

The herringbone tweed he was wearing was as much a piece of art as the pinstripe of yesterday had been, and it had probably cost as much as Darcy's entire wardrobe. "It's all right," she conceded. "It's just that—"

"Then I'll see you later. I'm only the backdrop, anyway. The bride is the most important thing." And Trey was gone.

The head of women's clothing was flipping through the contents of a rack, looking back and forth from the clothes to Darcy. The look on her face made it clear that she was in pain.

Probably it's the sight of my jeans, Darcy thought. *Maybe I should have turned out in my bathrobe and really given her a thrill.*

Then she looked more closely at the rack. Most of the things hanging there looked less like something a bride would choose and more like the suits she would select for her grandmother to wear to the wedding. There were ruffles and frills galore, and Darcy wouldn't be surprised if somewhere there was a table full of hats to match.

"Aren't these all just a little…" Darcy paused and tried to find a suitable word. "Formal?"

"We presumed that Mr. Kent's fiancée would have a certain level of sophistication," Arabella said without taking her eyes off the suit she'd obviously chosen. It was pale pink.

Sophistication. Well, that was one word for it, Darcy supposed.

Jason sighed. "Get going, Arabella. I'm sure this will take a while."

Justine waved Darcy over to the makeup table, flipped on a bank of lights that made Darcy wince and reached for a card of foundation colors to hold up next to her face. "You might want to make sure the boss has a photo of you to carry in his wallet," she said under her breath.

Darcy shot her a look. "Why?"

"Because I asked him what color your hair was and—typical male that he is—he said it was sort of brown. Very unhelpful. That's why Arabella brought everything in the women's department."

"Everything? You mean that's the whole selection?"

"Well, not literally. But she's got every size and color, just in case."

"Because he had no idea what size I am, either?"

Justine grinned. "He just told Arabella you were a nice armful."

The very idea of Trey Kent thinking of her as a nice armful, when he'd never even had an arm around her, made Darcy feel warm along the edges. With irritation, she told herself.

But she did have to admit that the man could think on his feet.

When the advertising manager showed Darcy into the jewelry department two hours later, the cameras were already set up and Trey was waiting, with one elbow propped on a tall case, talking to a man who was wearing magnifying glasses. He lifted a casual hand when Darcy came in.

Jason curtly introduced her to the art director, who was working to set up lights, and then he turned his attention to the cameras, snapping out directions.

Darcy, with nothing to do for the moment but wait, crossed the room to join Trey. The room's thick carpet, combined with a tightly cut skirt and a set of heels twice the height of anything she normally wore, made walking difficult. Fortunately, Trey seemed too absorbed in his conversation to notice how awkward Darcy was being.

Or perhaps he noticed but he's trying to ignore it, she thought.

Safely across the room, she leaned gratefully against a

glass case and held up her insulated mug in a half salute. "Thanks for sending up the coffee, Trey."

Trey shrugged. "Sorry it was only the regular stuff, not the fancy kind you wanted."

"This morning, it wouldn't have mattered." Darcy looked around the department. She was startled to see that the photographic equipment was just about the only thing in the whole section of the store—except for the plush carpet—that looked modern. The chandeliers were obviously antique, and the dark wood and glass cabinets could have been transplanted whole from the very first Kentwells store. Even the man Trey had been talking to—apparently the manager of the jewelry department—looked as if he could have been working there for a hundred years.

She couldn't help but wonder whether the merchandise matched the surroundings. But a glance told her that nearly everything inside the cases was the newest and brightest.

The department manager waved off an assistant who was trying to straighten his bow tie and with a flourish pulled out a tray of rings.

The cameramen moved closer, and Jason came up next to Darcy, clearing his throat. "Just look at the jewelry for right now," he said, "while we get the camera angles right. Then we'll have you do a little ooh and ahh routine before we get down to serious posing."

Darcy looked down at the tray. The stones caught the bright photo lights and fractured the beams into rainbows. "Ooh and ahh?" she said. "Over these?"

Jason frowned. "You have a problem with that?"

Darcy caught herself. The woman she was supposed to portray—the kind who would be marrying Andrew Patrick Kent the Third—would probably be drooling over this display. "Not at all," she said sweetly. "I can ooh and ahh with the best of them."

"Good. Because all of this was decided long ago. Every

ring in this selection is here because it'll make a striking photograph, and it's too late to be making extensive changes to the plan.''

Darcy smothered a sigh. Without even glancing at the group of rings in the tray on the counter, she stretched out a hand and picked up the first one her fingertip touched. Only then did she look at it.

Of everything in the tray, it was probably the one she'd have chosen last. The diamond was eye-catching, Jason was right about that, though to her eyes it shone like an airport spotlight. But the setting was much more elaborate than the kind of thing she liked. The stone sat high above the face of the ring, held up by a cage of gold filigree. The prongs which held it were likely to catch on every loose thread, and the gold filigree would need cleaning every time she put on hand lotion.

That's what you get for not looking before you leap, she told herself. She slid the ring onto her finger and held up her hand to inspect it. ''Ooh,'' she said. ''Ahh.''

From the corner of her eye, she saw Trey bite back a smile. ''Don't hurt yourself by being overenthusiastic, Darcy. That's a good choice, though—it's probably the clearest and whitest stone in the whole group.''

Jason looked over her shoulder at the ring. ''*And* the most expensive.''

The man might as well have called her a gold digger, Darcy thought irritably. His tone made his opinion clear. ''Surely you're not worried about whether Trey can afford it,'' she murmured, and looked up at Trey with a smile. ''The more expensive the ring, the bigger your employee discount. Right?''

''Let's shoot,'' Jason said. ''I like that pose. Lay your hand against Trey's cheek, Darcy, look up at him, and let's have a nice kiss.''

CHAPTER FOUR

A KISS.

And of course it couldn't be just any kiss, either, Darcy thought irritably, because Jason seemed to be expecting the handsome-prince-awakening-sleeping-beauty scenario.

The truth was that first kisses were always problematic. Even in private, between people who knew and liked each other, the odds were good that a first kiss would be the awkward, nose-bumping sort. Add the same number of on-lookers as the average World Cup game, and it was almost guaranteed that things would go wrong. Colliding chins, grinding lips, clattering teeth—the only positive Darcy could think of was that since they were both past the teen-age years, there were no braces to get tangled together.

Of course, she reminded herself, nobody but she and Trey knew this actually was a first kiss. So it had better be good enough that nobody started to have suspicions now.

She wanted to groan. Trey couldn't have thought to warn her about this?

And what would you have done if he had, Darcy? Suggest that we practice?

Maybe she was glad he'd left it to be a surprise. Or perhaps the omission hadn't been on purpose—maybe it hadn't even crossed his mind that she might like to have a heads-up.

The fact was she should have seen this one coming all by herself. Showing an engaged couple kissing was an ob-vious pose, and as stereotypical as they came. It was right down Jason's alley, if it came to that. But it would also no doubt be a popular feature of the ad campaign and an eye-catching way to start the series.

Still, she felt an overwhelming urge to protest.

"Pictures of people kissing aren't always such a great idea," she pointed out. "They sound a lot better in theory than they actually look in the end result. Take Hollywood and all the gyrations they have to go through. Or didn't you ever notice that if both faces are going to show in the shot, the actors can't even really be looking at each other in their big kissing scene?"

Jason scowled at her. "Who's in charge here, Trey?"

"I was only saying," Darcy put in, "that if you're planning to run these pictures big, Jason, they're going to look like—"

"The kissing shots won't be big."

"Shots?" Darcy said slowly. "Plural?"

"Didn't Trey tell you anything at all?" Jason's tone held a note that Darcy thought might possibly be amusement, but was more likely contempt. "That's the unifying theme of the campaign. In each ad, there will be a small photo of the bride and groom kissing, along with the bigger shots of the exact things they're selecting."

Darcy held on to her temper. "Trey seems to have been too busy with other things to explain the details to me. But that's fine—let's get it done."

"Of course, if you don't want to..." Now there was no doubt about the scornful twist in Jason's tone.

"But of course I want to." Darcy let her voice go husky. "I'm just not used to having the event recorded for posterity, since I don't generally consider kissing to be an audience-participation sort of event." She put one hand—the left one with the diamond ring snuggled at the base of her finger—against Trey's face as Jason had instructed, and the other against his chest.

His skin was warm and surprisingly soft, and the barest

hint of stubble on his jaw made her palm prickle. As his chest rose and fell, the silk of his tie caressed her fingertips, and she could feel the steady beat of his heart under her hand.

He put both arms around her, and despite her best intentions Darcy's muscles twitched in apprehension. It was such a small movement that she didn't think Jason or anyone on the crew could have noticed, but it was apparent Trey did, because he looked down at her with a shadow of sudden doubt in his eyes.

He was having second thoughts, obviously. She wondered if he was wishing that he'd warned her, or that he'd have preferred to have someone else in his arms right now. Whichever it was, it was too late for changes—but she was a bit irritated at his last-minute dubiousness.

So you think I can't do this? Darcy wanted to say. *Well, let me show you a thing or two, Mr. Kent.*

He must have seen the light of challenge in her eyes, because a sudden glint sprang to life in his—but by then Darcy had already started to move, and she'd committed herself. She raised herself onto her toes, let her hand trail down his cheek, held her breath for luck and pressed her lips against his.

Trey was absolutely still, as if shocked beyond measure at her forwardness.

Darcy was surprised at his lack of response. The man had already shown some natural acting ability, so surely he wasn't suffering a sudden attack of stage fright. Was he made of ice? Or was he deliberately causing the very sort of suspicion he'd said he wanted to avoid?

Dammit, she thought, *there's a principle at stake here. The least you could do is help me out.*

Darcy let her eyes drift closed, summoned all the warmth and soft appeal she could and kissed him as if she were welcoming her lover home from the far end of the universe.

If she'd kept her eyes open, she might have had an instant's warning—though it probably wouldn't have made any difference in the outcome, because the millisecond Trey moved, she lost all pretense of controlling the situation.

Trey's arms tightened around her, lifting her off her feet, and suddenly his mouth was hungry against hers. He kissed her until her breath ran out and she felt everything start to turn a little blue around the edges, and when he finally raised his head she couldn't force air back into her lungs because she couldn't seem to get control over her muscles. She thought she must sound as if she were wheezing her way out of an asthma attack, and hoped that it was only the unnatural silence around her, and her own skewed perceptions, which made it seem that way.

"Maybe we should just clear a space on the floor," one of the crew members muttered.

"Shut up," Jason told him. "Trey—Darcy—That looked awkward. You want to try it again, with a little more restraint?"

Trey hadn't loosened his grip. Which was probably a good thing, Darcy thought, or she'd be on the floor already and the crew would be getting even wilder ideas.

"Darcy did warn you that it might not be a good plan," Trey said. "And it's been—what, darling?—a couple of hours since our last kiss? The tension must have been building up, but I think now we can exercise a little more control. Ready, everybody?"

Darcy would have pleaded that she was far from prepared, but she couldn't get her voice to work right either. However, the second kiss was much cooler, more restrained and—she suspected—far more photogenic. At least she kept seeing flashes go off, despite the fact that she'd once more closed her eyes.

Or was that just the aftereffects of the first kiss? There

still seemed to be a lot of unexplained electrical pulses zooming through her body, setting off nerve fibers seemingly at random.

So much for standing on principle, Darcy, she told herself.

Trey was still holding her, she noticed. His arm was tightly wrapped around her waist and his hip was braced against one of the jewelry cases as if he were having trouble holding both of them upright. She'd have to put a stop to that—and firmly—before he concluded she was some kind of clinging vine, or simply too blown away by his skill to keep her balance.

She pushed herself half a step away from him, cleared her throat and said, "I'm sure that was good enough, so what's next?"

The art director shook his head. "Oh, no, that was just the test shot to check for lighting angles. We'll look that one over and adjust a few things, and then we'll get down to the real work."

"You mean we're going to be—" Darcy caught herself in the nick of time and bit her lip.

"Kissing all morning is a more pleasant occupation than some I could think of," Trey murmured. "Let's look at rings while they dissect the picture."

"Why?" She looked down at the tray of rings and shrugged. "They're all pretty much the same, you know. Big and round, big and square, big and pointed...."

"What's wrong with big diamonds?"

"Nothing at all, as long as they come with a crane to help carry them around."

Trey had folded his arms across his chest. "So if you don't like these, what do you like?"

"Not that it matters, but I'd start over there." She waved a hand at a case of old-looking jewelry.

"Those are antiques."

"They're one of a kind," Darcy said. "Unique and traditional. Showcasing the Kentwells stores' emphasis on family values, the continuity of the business, and your commitment to being here for generations to come. Customer service which lasts as long as the diamonds you sell."

Trey looked at her with an odd shimmer in his eyes. "Hey, that's not bad."

"I'll take care of the slogans, thank you." Jason's voice was impatient. "And they've already been decided for the whole campaign, remember? All right, we're ready to go."

"Darcy's not," Trey said. "She hasn't chosen her ring yet."

"She said it doesn't matter," Jason pointed out.

"And I say it does," Trey said.

While they were arguing about it, Darcy decided she'd just go and take a look. As she turned toward the case of antiques, her ankle wobbled, unaccustomed to the combination of high slim heels and deep plush carpet. She reached out for Trey's arm for support, and the prongs holding the immense diamond in the ring she was wearing caught the edge of his sleeve as she grabbed. It pulled out a long loop of tweed and skidded across the back of his hand, leaving a red welt. She looked up at him, horrified. "I'm sorry, Trey."

Trey thoughtfully surveyed the damage. "Well, that ring certainly left an impression." He rubbed his hand as he looked at the department manager. "Do we sell anything that isn't classified as a deadly weapon?"

"This," Jason said, not quite under his breath, "is what happens when you work with amateurs. They keep changing their minds."

Darcy was already looking at the case. Still half-blinded by the glitter of the display of engagement rings, her eyes took a moment to adjust to the quieter beauty of the antiques—necklaces and bracelets and earrings which had been worn and loved by generations past. There were fewer diamonds here and more colored stones—garnet and emerald and opal, and even cameos. The gold wasn't as shiny as in the new rings; its gleam had been softened by the patina of time. Some of the edges were rounded with wear, and there were fine scratches which were visible even without a magnifying lens.

Tucked into a corner of the case was a small box covered in worn blue plush. Inside was a gold band which looked like a lightweight twisted rope. Deeply set into the gold was an oval-cut amethyst. It was very plain, and very beautiful, and something about it drew not only her eye, but her heart.

"That one," Darcy said, and without a word the department head unlocked the case and handed her the box.

Jason peered over her shoulder and made a face. "Trey, we've already decided all this. We're wasting time."

"Yes, we are." Trey took the plush box out of Darcy's hand and set it on the glass top of the case.

She opened her mouth to protest. All she wanted to do was try the ring on, for heaven's sake. It would take a grand total of fifteen seconds. *Then* she'd play by the rules—she'd be a good girl just as he expected; she'd go back to the rack of diamonds and choose a big splashy one, and everybody would be satisfied. It wasn't as if she seriously thought he'd been doing anything except going through the motions when he'd said the choice was hers, when clearly it wasn't.

She'd just have to be more careful in the future about brushing against him with the prongs, that was all.

Trey reached for her hand. What was he going to do, Darcy wondered—drag her bodily back across the room? That would certainly look good for the accumulated audience.

Instead he tugged the big diamond from her finger and dropped it on the case. It hit the glass at an angle, spun in a slow circle and finally came to rest. But Trey was apparently paying no attention. He pulled the amethyst ring out of the box and slid it on to Darcy's finger.

"Trey," Jason said. "Any of the rings we've already chosen would look good. Better than that ever can."

"Are you saying your team is incapable of showing off any piece of jewelry in this department in a good light?" Trey wasn't looking at Jason but at the ring nestled at the base of Darcy's finger.

But Darcy saw the look on the advertising manager's face. "It doesn't matter, Trey," she said under her breath. "Let's just choose a diamond and move on."

"Yes, it does matter. You'll be wearing this for a long time, so you're going to select one you like. Is this it?" He held her hand up a bit higher to look at it.

You'll be wearing this for a long time. Darcy had to admit he was right—three months was starting to look like a very long time indeed.

The ring was so light that she'd almost forgotten she was wearing it. "I like it a lot," she admitted. "It's not a ball and chain like the other one was."

Trey ran the ball of his thumb over the amethyst. "And it's not as sharp as a fish-filet knife, either. This will do."

"There's no wedding ring to go with it," Jason said. "If you'd just be sensible and buy a set—"

Great. We have to buy a wedding ring even though we have no intention of using it.

The department head spoke up, the first time he'd said a word since Darcy had come in. "We can make one."

"Really?" Darcy said. "You mean right here? I had no idea you did that."

"And neither do the majority of our customers," Trey

said. "It'll give us another hook for an ad. See what a great idea this is, Jason? Now—let's get down to business. I've got a lunch date."

Darcy spent the rest of the photo shoot in a sort of daze. She must have done whatever Jason asked, because they moved steadily—though slowly—from closeups of her hand cradled in Trey's, showing off the amethyst, to rough sketches of a possible coordinating wedding ring. And eventually even Jason seemed satisfied. He dismissed the extra crew, and the photographers began to break down their equipment.

"That's it?" Darcy said under her breath.

"Personally, I've never worked so hard doing nothing before," Trey said. "We're done here, but we'll be shooting in the furniture department this afternoon."

"Oh, that's right. What time shall I be back?"

"Back? Where are you going?"

"Anywhere but here, for a while."

"You'll feel better after some food. Come on."

"You said you had a lunch date."

"I do. With you. Let's go up to The Restaurant."

Darcy hesitated. "Have they moved the clothes? Because if they haven't, I really don't want to look at those racks again."

"I'm sure they have. But if you'd rather go somewhere else…"

"Yes, please. Somewhere we can actually talk."

"I'm not sure I like the sound of that." But he tucked his hand under her elbow and guided her out of jewelry, past rare books and antiques and down the escalator to the mall entrance. "Is someplace in the food court all right with you?"

"I'd find something like potstickers to be comforting, yes. Or a nice big thick raspberry and banana smoothie."

"Oh, if those are the choices, then it definitely has to be the potstickers. Raspberries and bananas sound far too healthy to be truly comforting. What's the matter, anyway?"

"You know, you could warn me about these things ahead of time."

He looked surprised. "You were doing just fine."

Darcy opened her mouth, and then thought better of it. Why go looking for trouble by detailing her irritation? If she told him that she was not, in fact, doing just fine when it came to kisses and hugs for the camera, it would only encourage him to be suspicious about why. And he might conclude that her discomfort wasn't coming from inexperience at the modeling game but from something far more personal.

Something associated with him. Which was ridiculous, of course.

No, she'd just as soon not give him any reason to think about that. In any case, with the first—and worst—kiss out of the way, future photo opportunities would be neither a surprise nor something to dread. She'd be fine from here on out.

Yes, she told herself. The worst was over with.

Though Darcy had to admit, as kisses went, it hadn't been bad at all. In fact, if it hadn't been for the surroundings, the audience and the cameras, it might have been very pleasant indeed. Trey's kiss had certainly roused instincts deep within her which she'd thought were not just dormant but extinct.

And very foolish it would be to let that make a difference in her future conduct, she reminded herself. She'd made the mistake once of thinking that a man's charm meant he loved her. She'd thought Pete had cared about her, when he was only doing what was expedient at the moment. She wouldn't let that happen again—and the first step was to make it very clear to Trey that kissing him had made no impact on her at all.

"Thank you," she said politely. "I'm quite flattered to have your approval. What's Jason's problem, anyway? I've been around the business world for half a dozen years and I've never seen such a big chip on a shoulder before."

"He thought with my father out of the picture that he'd be taking over the store. Then I came back."

"So his nose is out of joint at not being the boss? I'm surprised you haven't fired him."

"I can't, exactly. He's a cousin."

"And a stockholder? That's a nice combination to have following you around and arguing all day."

"Keeps me on my toes. Potstickers, you said?" He held a chair for her in the open food court and went up to the counter to order.

The chair was less than comfortable—deliberately so, Darcy had always thought, in order to keep people from using the food court as a lounge—but she leaned back anyway, trying to ease the ache in her spine after the long morning of standing. She slid one foot out of her high-heeled shoe and rubbed the arch against her other ankle. Though she was trying to be discreet, the effort obviously wasn't working; she noticed that a young man at a nearby table was watching her with interest. He was sipping coffee while the two small children beside him concentrated on their lunch.

Two kids with him and he was eyeing a woman in the food court... *Some guys just never give up girl-watching.*

Trey came back with a huge basket and two drinks. "I took a chance and brought you something long and cold."

"Thanks. I hope it's sticky, too. Do me a favor and dump it on that guy over there."

"Which guy?" He looked casually around. "The one with the kids?"

"And the wedding ring so shiny it glares clear across the mall." Too late Darcy remembered Joe and the bar. "Never mind," she added hastily. "I don't want a food-court fight in my honor."

"Oh, it wouldn't bother me. My suit's already ruined." He lifted a casual hand in the direction of the young man with the kids, and then turned back to Darcy. "I'll be just a minute."

"No, really, don't go over there. It's not important." Darcy laid a hand on his arm to hold him back and tried to change the subject. "You know, I would offer to replace your suit, just because it seems to be the proper thing to do. However, since I can't begin to afford a suit of that caliber, and since it was a piece of your merchandise—which I didn't want to be wearing in the first place—which caused the damage, I…" Her voice trailed off. "Wait a minute. Did you just *wave* at the guy who was making eyes at me?"

"Yes, I waved. And no, he wasn't making eyes at you. He was just interested in who I was with."

"I noticed that part," Darcy said dryly.

"That's the chairman of the board of my competition."

"The head of the Tyler-Royale department store chain is having lunch in the mall food court?"

"Why shouldn't he? *I'm* having lunch in the food court—and he has a better excuse."

"You mean the kids?"

"Yes. While my only companion is…"

"…A woman who's acting like a child. All right, you've made your point. Shall I be haughty to him, or charming?"

"Oh, definitely charming. He's coming this way." Trey got to his feet. "Ross—good to see you, buddy. I'd like you to meet my fiancée."

The word sounded awkward on his tongue. Darcy figured it might be the first time he'd actually used it to a colleague, though perhaps he'd said it to an employee or two. It would be no wonder if it felt strange to him—it certainly sounded strange to her. Taking the news outside the Kentwells store made it sound more real somehow—and more serious.

She held out a hand to the man who had approached the table. He wasn't as young as he'd looked from a distance, she realized, and the expression in his eyes wasn't a come-on but genuine interest. Trey had been right.

"Congratulations, Trey," the man said. "And best wishes to the bride." He frowned a little. "Did I get that right, or is it the other way around? My wife will slice and dice me if I get the manners thing wrong."

"I have no idea," Darcy said. "I still have to buy an etiquette book so I can find out what's expected of me."

"I see you have the important things, though." He nodded toward the amethyst gleaming on her hand. "That looks like your grandmother's ring, Trey. Nice to meet you, Ms...."

"Darcy Malone," she said quickly.

"Ross Clayton. Trey, we must get together for a chat sometime." He shook hands again, and walked away.

Trey was frowning, Darcy noted. "What was that all about?"

She thought for a minute that he wasn't going to answer at all. "Coupon reciprocity," he said finally.

Darcy rolled her eyes. "You mean like the Kentwells store accepting Tyler-Royale coupons at face value, and vice versa? Sure it was—and I'm the Easter Bunny, too. Either you don't know what he wanted, or you don't want to tell me. I can take a hint, Trey."

"That's the first I'd seen of it," he murmured.

"By the way, do you suppose he intended that to be a nasty crack? About this looking like your grandmother's ring, I mean."

"I doubt it. It's just a fact. Have a potsticker."

Darcy reached for one, and then let her hand fall short of the basket. "Wait a minute. It's just a fact? You actually put *your grandmother's* ring up for sale in the store?"

Trey frowned. "That's not what I said."

"But this *is* your grandmother's ring?"

"No—it's just a style that looks like it could be. Half the women of her generation had something like that."

"Oh." Darcy relaxed. "Sorry. I jumped to a conclusion there, I guess."

"That's your favorite form of exercise, I've noticed—jumping to conclusions."

Darcy bit her lip. She did seem to be making a habit of wrong deductions lately, especially where Trey was concerned. Though why she should be surprised, considering the circumstances.... "Well, it wouldn't have surprised me if it had been a rude comment," she said in her own defense. "If not about the ring, then about the suit I'm wearing. Half of your grandmother's generation had clothes like this, too."

"It's not one of Arabella's better choices," Trey said.

"No kidding. I think Jason was in favor, though. You did say you'd pay me for the time I spend doing these pictures, right?"

"I believe I did tell you that. Why?"

"Because there's a sale going on down at the other end of the mall today, and I'd like to wander through and take a look. If you could advance me a little money—"

"You're not serious. You want to go shopping at the competition's store?"

"Yes, I do. At least then I'd have something I actually want to wear."

"Something to wear in photos for Kentwells ads? Dammit, Darcy—"

"I don't suppose Jason would like it much."

"Like it? Honey, you've succeeded in doing something

I thought couldn't be managed at all—putting Jason and me on the same side of a question. Why shop with the competition, anyway? Why not look around our store?''

"Our store," she said contemplatively. "It has such a nice ring to it, Trey. I could grow fond of the idea of community property." She noticed the clouds gathering in his eyes and decided it was time to stop teasing. "If I go shopping at Kentwells, I have to deal with Arabella."

"I'll pull Arabella off so you can choose what you like."

"Thanks, Trey."

He smiled then. "You're not a bad little negotiator, Darcy. Threatening me with a shopping spree at Tyler-Royale to get what you want at Kentwells... Nice move."

She decided it wouldn't be prudent to tell him that it hadn't exactly been a ploy. "How does my employee discount work?" she asked instead.

"Just sign the receipts and send them to my office."

"Oh, that sounds like fun. Not that I expect to find enough clothes I like to cause you to lose any sleep over your charge account."

"Not mine," he said crisply. "Believe me, I'll be keeping track."

"Skinflint. But that's okay—Tyler-Royale always has great coupons in their ads, and as long as you're going to honor them...." Darcy reached for a potsticker. "If you and Jason really disagree all the time, how did you both manage to approve of on this wedding promotion? Whose idea was it, anyway?"

"Caroline's, I believe," Trey said. "Or rather it was Corbin's. He wanted to have his business qualifications splashed all over each ad."

"And get some free stuff along the way, I suppose. Well, that explains everything. I thought Caroline was the only family you had."

"Not quite. You and I have a date for tea this evening with my great-aunt."

"I thought tea was an afternoon event."

"Tea is whenever Aunt Archie wants to have it."

That sounded threatening. "Aunt Archie?"

"Millicent Archibald. The grapevine seems to have notified her that there's going to be a wedding in the family, and she wants to meet the bride."

Darcy looked at him in disbelief. "The grapevine told her? You didn't even call her up to tell her yourself? Maybe we should get two copies of that etiquette book, because you could sure use one."

"I didn't think about calling her."

"At least it's a comfort to know that you didn't actually try to swear everybody to secrecy so she wouldn't find out until she saw the first ad in the newspaper. You know, you appear to be determined to make people not believe in this engagement."

He seemed not to hear her. Which might be just as well, Darcy thought. "Trey? Are you still irritated at me over wanting to shop at Tyler-Royale instead of your store?"

"Hmm? No, of course not. Tea's at seven."

"I suppose this outfit will do?"

Trey checked his wristwatch. "It will have to, because there's no time to go shopping right now. We're supposed to be doing the furniture department this afternoon."

"Oh, that's great," Darcy murmured. "Because I can't wait to see Jason's face when I start bouncing on mattresses in this skirt."

CHAPTER FIVE

BOUNCING on the mattress, trying it out... It was no more than an idle threat, Trey told himself. Darcy wouldn't actually do it. Would she?

No, he reassured himself, of course she wouldn't. No matter how much of an instant dislike she'd taken to Jason, she wouldn't make herself look a fool just for the sake of seeing the expression on the advertising manager's face.

And rolling around on a mattress in that skirt—which was tightly cut and bound to ride up around her hips the instant she moved—would indeed make her look like a fool.

Unless, of course, it just made her look sexy as hell instead, to display every inch of her elegant slim legs encased in sheer hose that seemed to go on forever...

Trey's gaze had gone straight to her legs when she'd come into the jewelry department this morning. The last thing he'd have expected yesterday when she walked into his life was that those baggy sweatpants were concealing the greatest set of legs of the decade, and he wondered if she had any idea what an asset she was hiding. Probably not—so if she did the mattress-bouncing test, it sure wouldn't be because she was hoping to get a reaction from him. Only from Jason.

No surprise there, really, since the advertising manager had been anything but charming this morning. Still, the idea that Darcy would go to any lengths to raise Jason's hackles, while not giving a damn about what Trey thought, irritated him. Of course, that was the deal they'd made—but he hadn't expected that she'd pay so much attention to his cousin.

Even the way she'd kissed Trey had very little to do with him, he thought. She'd flung herself at him like a nymphomaniac just to see Jason's reaction.

For an instant there, he'd been taken aback—until he'd realized what she was up to. But he'd showed her in the end that he wasn't to be trifled with like that. She'd been the one to start the little game, but by the time he'd ended it, she hadn't been so sanguine. She'd been out of breath and barely able to stand up, and he'd have bet his next profit-sharing check that she hadn't been thinking about Jason any longer.

Yes, he'd certainly made his point there—even if doing so had left him nearly as short of oxygen and weak in the knees as she'd seemed to be.

So if she got too outrageous, he'd just kiss her again. That would keep both her and Jason toeing the line, and Trey wouldn't mind a bit. Next time he'd just remember to take a couple of very deep breaths first.

He'd been right last night about how dangerous it would be to seduce her. A woman who didn't yak all the time, who kissed like an angel, who fitted in his arms and under his chin…. And one who couldn't resist a challenge. In the long run, that might be a handy thing to know—that she couldn't turn down a dare. But why was she so set on proving something to Jason? And what?

Trey very deliberately stopped thinking about Jason— there was no sense wasting mental fuel on someone he couldn't change—and turned his attention back to Ross Clayton instead. What had the CEO of a major department store chain been doing at the mall food court in the middle of a Wednesday instead of in his corporate office downtown?

Taking a day off with his kids, of course. It would be

stupid to read hidden meanings into his mere presence. If he wanted to talk to Trey, he could walk from the food court down to the store, or pick up the phone.

Still, it had been an odd comment that Ross had made. *We must get together for a chat sometime...* Had it been only the sort of casual, almost meaningless time-filler that showed up in so many business conversations? Had Ross perhaps just been talking about the occasional need for mall merchants to show a united front? Or had he meant something more?

It was funny that Darcy had picked up on that question, too. With no experience in the trade, no previous acquaintance with Ross Clayton and not much familiarity with Trey's own body language, she'd still known instantly that there was something different going on.

Or at least, that Trey had thought there was something different going on.

Coupon reciprocity was the first thing that had popped into his head, and the sheer weirdness of the answer would have stopped most questioners dead in their tracks. Not Darcy, though. There was nothing wrong with the woman's brain, or her instincts when it came to marketing. He'd better not forget that.

Take, for instance, her threat to go shopping at the competition's store...she'd had him going for a minute there. He'd have to remember that line to toss at Jason sometime when the man was being particularly annoying...

He wondered what she thought was so much better about the store at the far end of the mall than his own, and started to make a mental list of possibilities—because the exercise was much more conducive to his peace of mind than if he let himself think about kissing her again.

Though, of course, it was going to be important to keep her off balance—no matter what it took to do the trick.

Maybe he'd damn the torpedoes and seduce her after all. What was life worth, anyway, without a little danger to spice it up now and then?

Despite being subjected to the interested gaze of Trey's secretary, Darcy almost dozed off while sitting outside his office, reading the newspaper and waiting for him to get clear of the last-minute paperwork which had built up through the afternoon.

What was it he'd said after the morning photo session, about never before having worked so hard to accomplish nothing? He'd been right on target there, she thought. She was exhausted, and there was still the evening—and tea with Aunt Archie—to go.

When Trey finally reappeared, Darcy glanced at the clock on the far wall and raised her eyebrows at him. "Let's make plain to your aunt that it's not my fault we're late."

"Sorry it took me so long," he announced.

"All right, then." Darcy waved the colorful ad supplement she'd been reading at the secretary and tucked it under her arm. "Thanks for the paper, Carol."

Trey paused with the office door half-open. "Why are you taking that ad section with you?"

"Because I believe it leaves the wrong impression to have it lying around your waiting room."

He ushered her out into the narrow hall and stopped. "Now that Carol can't hear you, how about giving me the real reason?"

Darcy smiled at him. "Very well. Because I haven't quite read it from cover to cover yet."

"I thought we'd agreed you weren't going to be shopping at Tyler-Royale, so why do you need to look at their ad?"

"Coupon reciprocity," she said sweetly. "They've scheduled a half-off sale for Saturday, and I can't wait to spring the idea on Arabella. What held you up all this time, anyway? Were there more phone calls from disappointed former girlfriends than you expected?''

"No. Why?''

"Because I figured if it was merely business, you'd have your secretary take care of it rather than be late to tea with your aunt. Personal matters, on the other hand, would require your own touch to soothe the troubled waters, and by now, the word must be getting out that you're no longer in circulation. However, if you'd rather not talk about that, I'll just finish reading the ads.''

"Give me that." He made a grab for the paper.

"If you insist, of course you can have it." Darcy handed it over. "Are you looking for any item in particular?— because maybe I can tell you which page it's on.''

Trey crumpled the flyer and pitched it into a garbage bin.

"I see. Well, I'll just pick up another copy. In fact, I wonder…if I stopped by to see the chairman, do you suppose he'd give me an extra coupon or two?''

Trey smiled. "Feel free, but his office is in the flagship store downtown. I don't know why he was here today, but it didn't seem to be official business. Maybe he was taking his kids to visit Santa Claus.''

"In September?''

Trey shrugged. "The Christmas retail season starts earlier every year.''

Darcy rolled her eyes and let him hold the door of Caroline's car for her.

Millicent Archibald's house was not far from the mall, so they weren't very late after all. The house was straight out of classic literature, Darcy thought—a large but perfectly scaled Georgian gem built of gray and white stone with a Palladian window in the front facade, an unusually large and well-manicured lot, and a butler in a tailored black suit standing by to open the front door the moment the car stopped in the half-circle driveway.

. "Hello, sir," the butler said in a not-quite-nasal tone. "Madame is waiting in the drawing room. This way, miss."

"Hello, Gregory," Trey said, and the butler showed them into what could only be called a drawing room. A fire crackled on the hearth, a tea cart weighed down by a massive silver service stood in place nearby, and on a brocade pillow comfortably near the flames lay a blue-eyed Persian cat so perfectly combed and posed that he looked stuffed.

Darcy straightened her shoulders and took a firm grip on her manners. It was obvious that tea with Trey's great-aunt was going to be even more of an ordeal of perfection than she'd anticipated. No wonder Trey hadn't been eager to tell her about his engagement...

Exactly ten seconds too late, Darcy realized that she should have asked Trey what to call the woman. Not Aunt Archie, surely—the younger generation might call her that behind her back, but the woman who had drawn together the room, the tea cart, the silver service, the butler and the cat surely wouldn't welcome a nickname like that one. Well, she'd have to play it by ear.

She stepped forward onto a priceless Persian carpet, got her first good look at the woman rising from the couch to greet them, and blinked in surprise.

This wasn't at all what she'd expected. Darcy had drawn such a clear picture in her mind of a fluffy round woman with blue-toned hair and a pastel designer suit and pearls, looking down her nose at newcomers, that for a moment she thought she was hallucinating.

Millicent Archibald could certainly look down her nose. One of the tallest women Darcy had ever encountered, she was nearly the same height as Trey. But no other part of Darcy's mental picture held true. Lean and lanky, Trey's aunt was wearing khaki slacks with a shapeless red sweater, neon-yellow socks, and a tennis bracelet in which each diamond in the row must have been a half-carat in size. Her hair wasn't blue-toned and fluffy; it was black and gray and white in random streaks, and it looked as if she'd twisted it up in a knot that morning, nailed it to the back of her head with a handful of hairpins, and forgotten entirely to look in a mirror.

But her gaze was every bit as penetrating as the one Darcy had expected from the fluffy pastel person of her imagination. Millicent Archibald tipped her head back, narrowed her eyes, and surveyed Darcy from head to painfully pinched toes. "She's absolutely perfect, Trey." Her voice sounded almost rusty. "Just what I would have expected of you."

Darcy was reasonably certain that wasn't intended to be a compliment. But she decided to play dumb for the moment, and she smiled and said, "Thank you, Madame."

"Gregory!" the woman bellowed. "Now you're infecting other people! How many times have I told you not to call me that hideous name?"

The butler bowed from the door. "Is that a rhetorical question, Madame?"

"Oh, go away and bring some food in here." She settled back on the couch. "Call me Archie—everybody does except Gregory." Her bright eyes came to rest once more on Darcy. "So you're going to be the Kentwells bride. A bit of a sudden change, that."

"How did you hear about it?" Trey asked.

"Caroline called me to ask if she could have the engagement party here. I invited her and Corbin for tea, too, but she said she couldn't come." She waved a hand at the tea cart and looked at Darcy. "You pour tea, of course?"

Did she pour tea? What kind of a question was that?

A tricky one—Darcy was dead sure of it. What she didn't

know was quite where the trick lay. Certainly there must be more to the business of pouring tea than shifting liquid from a pot to a cup, or Aunt Archie wouldn't have said it in quite that tone of voice—as if it were some sort of a test.

Darcy shot what she hoped was a surreptitious look at the tea cart. The silver service loomed even larger as she stared at it. There were multiple pots—big, little, and middle-sized. There was a jug of what looked like milk, a bowl obviously full of sugar, and a container which held nothing at all, as far as Darcy could see.

Not that it mattered much, for Aunt Archie hadn't waited for an answer. "Good," she said. "I never could manage it gracefully, so I'll happily turn the job over to you."

Darcy tried to catch Trey's eye, but he seemed oblivious. She swallowed hard and settled behind the tray. "How do you like your…"

"Oh, just fill a cup from the small pot for me, dear. Nothing else."

The silver pot was unexpectedly heavy, considering how small it was. It wobbled in Darcy's grip and without thinking she steadied it with her other hand, leaving—she instantly saw—a perfectly pristine fingerprint on the glossy surface. She sighed and figured she'd gotten off lucky as it was, not burning herself by grabbing at the pot that way. But in fact, it had felt chilly to the touch… Was it the upper-crust thing to do to serve iced tea in a silver pot rather than in a pitcher?

"Never mind, dear," Aunt Archie said. "The fingerprint, I mean. It'll give Gregory something to feel superior about, and he does so appreciate the opportunity."

Darcy filled a cup. An unusual aroma rising from the liquid caught at her senses and she sniffed. That, she thought, was the oddest-smelling tea she'd ever run across.

Trey scooped up the cup and saucer and took it to Aunt

Archie, who sipped and smiled. "I figure I'm making enough of a concession by using the antique silver and china," she said. "But I draw the line at rotting my insides with Earl Grey. Give me good old Kentucky bourbon any day of the week. Shocked, my dear? Well, you'll get used to it—or else we won't get along very well."

"Frankly," Darcy said, "at the moment, I'd rather have the bourbon, too."

Aunt Archie let out a delighted-sounding bray. "So you're not just another inflatable doll lookalike after all. Where did he find you?"

"Trey and my brother are old friends," Darcy said sedately.

"The suit threw me for a minute, though, I have to admit. I'm amazed at you, Trey—not having the girl out of those clothes before now."

Darcy's face suddenly felt hotter than the largest of the teapots. Aunt Archie couldn't possibly have intended that to sound suggestive—so why was Darcy abruptly having visions? Trey dealing competently with buttons and ties; Trey's fingertips running along her skin as he eased the silky blouse off her shoulders; Trey tracing the line of the plain white bra Arabella had chosen for her—and with his touch turning it into the sexiest garment Darcy had ever worn...

She took a deep breath and focused on pouring bourbon into a second tea cup without splashing, and then risked a glance at Trey. He was looking at her thoughtfully, as if contemplating what Aunt Archie had said, and she felt a shiver run down between her breasts as if he'd touched her. "What would you like, Trey?" Mercifully her voice didn't catch.

He seemed in no hurry to answer, but he finally said lazily, "To drink?"

Her face grew even hotter.

"Not booze in a cup, that's for sure," he went on. "And not tea, either. Archie thinks I'm a snob, but I prefer my scotch in a glass, with ice." He strolled over to a cabinet at the end of the room and poured himself a drink.

"Oh, goodness." Aunt Archie's bright gaze was fixed on Darcy's face. "Don't mind me, my dear, I'm always sticking my foot in my mouth. Good thing it's so big, right?" She demonstrated with an enormous smile. "All I meant was that I haven't seen anyone under the age of eighty wearing something like that suit in the last three decades."

Darcy felt a measure of relief—though unfortunately, her skin was still reacting to the heat of Trey's imaginary touch. "I told you," she muttered to Trey.

"Trey, take the girl shopping, for heaven's sake. And while you're at it, buy yourself some yellow socks." Aunt Archie held up one foot, displaying her own neon footwear. "You can't take yourself so seriously if you're wearing yellow socks."

The butler came in with another tray, loaded with a variety of snack foods, and set it on the low table in front of Aunt Archie. "Take the tea away, Gregory," she said. "Nobody here wants it, so you may as well take it back to the kitchen and drink it while it's hot."

"And the scones, Madame?"

"Oh, you can leave those. The cat likes the clotted cream."

As if he'd been listening, the cat raised his head from the pillow, then stood up and stretched gracefully.

"No brain," Aunt Archie said. "I don't know why I keep him around. I'm talking about the cat, Gregory, not you. Hey, don't take away my personal pot—just the tea." As the butler left the room, she sat back on the couch, her teacup cradled in her hand. "So what's the real story here?"

Darcy's hand froze on her cup.

"I don't think Trey's been jealous of the attention Caroline was getting over being the featured bride. So what's the scoop?" Aunt Archie's bright gaze flashed from one to the other. "Not talking? All right. Let's see your ring, dear."

Darcy held out her hand.

Aunt Archie inspected the amethyst and sniffed. "Now that's what I call cheap, Trey. Passing off a recycled ring and calling it special, instead of buying a new one."

"This is what I wanted," Darcy said.

"Then you need your head examined, girl. Grab the biggest diamond you can get."

"Is that where your tennis bracelet came from?" Darcy asked.

"Hell, no. After my first divorce, I pawned the rock my ex-husband gave me, started up a business, and bought the bracelet with my first few months' profits." She reached for a handful of chips from a basket on the food tray. "I recommend it. A business is much more reliable than a man."

"Not a bad idea," Darcy admitted. "I'm starting a business myself, as soon as the photography's finished for this ad campaign. A little graphics design firm. Trey's going to give me his account."

"Good timing," Aunt Archie said. "Take advantage of the publicity. And there's nothing wrong with a little creative nepotism, either. I've always believed in it. If the amethyst isn't enough to get you started, dear, come and talk to me."

Darcy's head was still spinning and she felt a bit limp when Gregory ushered them out. She sank into the cushiony seat of Caroline's sports car and stared at the moon, just rising over the roof of Millicent Archibald's house. "Trey, did any of that really happen?"

"Aunt Archie tends to take people that way. They're either completely enchanted or totally incensed."

"Yeah, I can understand that reaction. Both of them." She sat up straighter. "My car is still at the mall, you know."

"You're sure you're all right to drive? Drinking bourbon from a teacup makes it difficult to judge how much you've actually had."

"Not enough to impair my judgment. And before you ask how on earth I could possibly tell, since my judgment's always impaired—"

"I didn't say a word," Trey protested.

"What kind of business was your aunt Archie in? It must have been a good one if the first few months' profits paid for that bracelet. At least fifty stones, half a carat apiece—it makes those rings Jason chose look pretty cheap."

"Public relations."

Darcy gasped. "*Aunt Archie* went around polishing people's images? You're not serious."

"Of course I'm not serious. That was a test to see whether you'd lost all perspective yet. I'm glad to see you haven't."

"So what did she really do?"

"She ran an insurance agency. All she had to do was set foot in a businessman's office, and he'd sign the paperwork for a half-million dollars worth of whole life just to get rid of her."

"That's not a kind thing to say, Trey."

"Maybe not, but it's true. And that bit about nepotism—everybody in the family's worth more dead than alive because of Aunt Archie. Except, just possibly, Archie herself." He pulled Caroline's car into the mall lot and stopped beside Darcy's compact. "You're sure you're all right to drive home? I can take you, and pick you up in the morning.''

Darcy gave him her most stunning smile. ''No need. I want to get an early start tomorrow to scope out all the merchandise at Tyler-Royale.''

''Darcy—''

''Not to buy anything,'' she assured him. ''Only so I know whether the prices at Kentwells are fair. See you in the morning.'' She shut the car door before he could answer.

Since she was a great deal later than usual, she expected the cottage to be dark. Mrs. Cusack would long since have covered her computer and gone home, and Dave would have made his regular pilgrimage to the post office and then probably stopped at Tanner's for a beer or gone to see Ginger...

Ginger. Darcy's own voice came back to her with the thump of a hammer inside her skull. *''Why don't you invite Ginger over for dinner tonight?''* she had asked Dave just this morning. *''I can warm up takeout Chinese with the best of them.''*

The memory came back to her at the very instant she turned the corner nearest the cottage and saw light flooding from the front windows of both the reception room and the law library. Either business was brisk and Dave was seeing clients in a rare night session, or Darcy was toast with her brother's girlfriend.

She didn't realize she'd actually stopped her car in the middle of the street until the driver behind her tapped on the horn. Only then did she check her mirror and realize that it was Caroline's red sports car behind her. Trey had followed her.

She pulled up to the curb and got out, waiting impatiently until he'd parked. Then she walked up to the driver's side window. "Forget something?" she asked. "Or did you think I'm so addled I couldn't find my way home?"

"Aunt Archie has that effect on people sometimes. But now that I'm here—what's going on? A party?"

"Sure," she said blithely. "While you were in your office returning calls from old girlfriends, I was summoning every guy I ever dated to a gang celebration tonight."

"Will there be pizza?"

Darcy gave up. There was absolutely no point in trying to pull his chain when he was three steps ahead of her to start with. "Honestly, Trey, how should I know what's going on? Dave's entertaining Ginger, I suppose."

"With all the lights on?"

"That just shows where your mind migrates."

She thought he was trying—without much success—to smother a grin. "Well, yes, I'm afraid it does. Even if he's not interested in marrying her, she must hold some sort of attraction for him."

"And what else could there possibly be besides sex? Common literary interests? Hobbies? Brilliant conversation?"

"Would you care to put five bucks on the question?"

"Oh, forget I said anything. See you tomorrow."

"You're a coward. I'll walk you in."

"Not necessary."

"What if it's not Dave after all?"

"Then maybe it's Mrs. Cusack holding a lingerie party. I doubt it's a burglars' convention because all the lights are on, and since Dave doesn't have any clients accused of spying, it's probably not the FBI, either. I'll be fine."

Trey got out of the car. "Personally, I'm hoping for the lingerie party."

"Obviously you've never met Mrs. Cusack or you wouldn't be daydreaming about seeing her in a red lace teddy."

"Lingerie," Trey added thoughtfully. "I wonder if that's on the list for us to shop for."

"It would be just my luck if Arabella still stocks whalebone corsets," Darcy muttered. She unlocked the front door and pushed it open cautiously. "Dave? I'm home. Look, I'm really sorry I didn't call to tell you I'd be late. I know we sort of had dinner plans with Ginger, but things happened and it slipped my mind and—"

She stopped in midbreath as she took in the scene in the reception room. Dave was sitting at one end of the couch, with a wineglass in his hand and a legal pad on his lap, and in front of him, squarely in the center of the carpet, stood a woman. She was a redhead, though Darcy was pretty sure she hadn't been born that way, and she looked about nineteen. She was wearing a miniskirt which appeared to have been sized for a fashion doll rather than a human, tall black boots, and a leather jacket. Her hands were braced on her hips, but she craned her head to stare at Darcy. "Dinner plans?" she said. "With Ginger, did you say?"

"Well, yes. Sort of," Darcy said feebly. "And you must be Ginger, right?"

The woman nodded. "But this is the first I've heard about dinner plans."

"Well, it was only a casual, maybe-you-should-invite-Ginger…" *You're only making this worse, Darcy.* But she couldn't seem to bite her tongue hard enough. "So if you didn't come for dinner, Ginger, why are you here?"

"I drove past, and there was a woman here. I had to go around the block to park, and now Dave tells me she was just a client."

"I told you that because she *was* a client," Dave put in. "Which means I can't give you any more details, like name, address and marital status. Besides, she's not here now. Let me walk you out, Ginger." He put the legal pad face-down on the coffee table next to his wine glass and stood up.

Darcy stepped aside. Ginger appeared reluctant, but Dave's hand on her arm urged her toward the door.

As soon as they were out of sight, Trey turned to Darcy. "I think you owe me five bucks."

"I didn't realize the red light district had a preschool division." Darcy collapsed on the couch.

"How long has he been dating—that?" Trey asked politely.

"I hope it's long enough to realize it was a mistake. He might be giving her marching orders right now."

"I suppose there's no harm in wishful thinking."

"Thanks for popping my balloon." Darcy leaned back and held up one foot to unfasten the strappy sandal. "I'm going to tell Arabella I was mugged and the shoes were stolen."

"You like them that much?"

"Idiot. I never want to wear them again." She stretched out her leg. Her newly freed toes bumped a half-full wine-glass which was sitting on the carpet, just out of sight under the edge of the coffee table, and knocked it over. Red wine splashed into a pattern of jewel-like drops over the carpet nap.

Darcy looked thoughtfully from the spilled glass to the half-full one sitting on the table. Two glasses…and one of them had obviously been hastily—and not very safely—concealed. But why? Even though Ginger didn't seem the sort to understand the fine points of helping a client relax with a glass of wine, why had Dave tried to hide it?

The door of Dave's office creaked and from the corner of her eye Darcy saw a shadow lean out and then duck back into the office.

Dave came inside. "Sorry about that," he said. "Ginger gets a little possessive from time to time."

"I'd say," Darcy murmured. "By the way, your client—the one you told Ginger was gone—is getting restive back in your office."

Dave sighed. "I was afraid of that. You might as well come out," he called. "There are only friends here now."

Darcy tried not to be obvious about staring. But when the client came out of Dave's office, peeking around the corner first as if to be certain it was safe, Darcy felt her jaw go lax. "Caroline?" she gasped. "What are you doing here?"

Caroline turned pink. "Planning your engagement party."

Darcy flipped over the legal pad that Dave had so carefully placed face-down so Ginger couldn't see the contents. No doubt about it—there, in neat script that she didn't recognize, was a caterer, a menu, a band…

This was getting out of hand. She shot a look of appeal at Trey.

"Great idea," Trey said. "I assume you're working on the guest list, too. Add Ross Clayton for me, will you, Caroline?"

"Fantastic idea," Darcy muttered. "When I see him at the party, I can hit him up to be a customer when I get my business going."

"Darcy—"

"Now I really have to stop at Tyler-Royale in the morning," she went on. "Because I need to take another good look at their logo, so I can get to work on designing them a better one."

CHAPTER SIX

FOR a moment, the room was silent and the quartet formed a sort of rectangular standoff—Darcy sitting on the couch, Trey perched on the arm at the opposite end from her, Dave still with a hand on the door and Caroline hovering in the hallway between offices and reception room as if she were too ashamed of herself to come out.

Darcy took a closer look at Caroline. With only the artificial light as illumination, the shadow around Caroline's eye was even more pronounced, and the break in her lip looked even angrier than it had yesterday.

"Have you seen a doctor?" Darcy asked.

Caroline's fingertip went to her lip in a gesture which looked automatic.

"No, I stitched it up for her myself with sewing thread," Trey said. "Of course she saw a doctor."

"You know, Trey," Dave said easily, "maybe she'd like to answer questions herself. Caroline, sit down and finish your wine."

"That will be a little difficult." Darcy picked up the wineglass she'd kicked over. "I don't think it would taste too good if we tried to wring it out of the carpet. Is there any left in the bottle?"

Caroline's eyes widened. "I'm so sorry. I didn't mean—"

"Of course you didn't," Darcy said. "I didn't, either. I just didn't expect to find a glass of wine sitting under the table."

"It happens all the time," Dave put in.

Darcy stared at him for a moment in shock before she

realized that he was simply putting a very high-paying client at ease. "Look, Caroline," she said, "are you sure about throwing a party? I mean, if you didn't want Ginger to see you this way…"

Of course, Darcy had to admit that Ginger's reaction to the mere idea of Dave having a female client would likely have been enough to send any woman—no matter how healthy—fleeing for cover. But Caroline was obviously sensitive nonetheless. Aunt Archie had said Caroline had phoned her to ask about the party, and that she'd refused to come to tea in person. On the other hand, Darcy couldn't exactly blame Caroline for wanting to heal before she told Aunt Archie what had happened. Bad enough to have to tell her at all, but if Archie saw the evidence there would be no stopping her from sharing her opinions.

"Because if you're still talking about having it this weekend," Darcy said, "that's only a couple of days off. Unless you're planning to make it a costume party and wear a mask—"

Caroline smiled, carefully. "No—I'll be fine, Darcy, you'll see."

"Well, at least let me help with the organizing. Dave's helpless at this kind of thing, as I expect you found out. I'm not used to party planning, either, but I can certainly design an invitation. Just tell me what you want." *And I'll take all the time I can soak up to produce it, and maybe by that time we'll decide we don't need to throw a party after all.*

"There's no time to mail invitations," Caroline said. "So I've already started phoning all the guests."

It was too late to object, then. Darcy subsided into the couch. "Actually the masks sound like a great idea," she muttered. "I'll come as King Tut."

"I suppose I should have checked the times with you,"

Caroline went on. "But Dave said you didn't have any plans for Saturday night, and Trey had already…"

Trey moved suddenly and Caroline stopped in midsentence. It was the first time Darcy had ever seen the woman look awkward—as if she'd caught herself just on the brink of disaster.

Darcy wondered what she'd almost said. What was Trey supposed to be doing on Saturday night—and with whom? What plan had been sidetracked by this sudden engagement?

Not that it matters to me, she told herself. *It's just…interesting, that's all.*

Trey stood up. "I'll take you home, Caroline."

"I need to mop up that wine with club soda first, so the stain doesn't set."

"I'll take care of it," Dave said. "I'm the one who pushed the glass under the table."

"And I'll help," Darcy added. "I'm the one who kicked it over."

Caroline looked as if she didn't quite know what to think. She muttered something that Darcy didn't catch.

Trey turned to look at Darcy, and she was surprised to see warmth—maybe even something like gratitude—in his gaze. Was it just because she'd come to his sister's rescue instead of blaming her for the accident? And were the tears she saw rising to Caroline's eyes because she felt guilty over the wine stain or relieved not to be held responsible?

Darcy thought with a sudden rush of compassion that the damage Corbin had done to Caroline went much deeper than just a black eye and a split lip. The physical damage would heal in a few days—perhaps not in time for a weekend party as Caroline so clearly hoped, but soon. The other scars would take much longer.

Darcy crossed the room and gave the woman a hug. "Thanks for going to all the trouble for this party," she said. "It's sweet of you, when you have so much on your mind."

Caroline's smile was wobbly, and she didn't say anything. Dave helped Caroline into her coat, and a couple of minutes later, Darcy heard the familiar soft roar of the sports car as it pulled away from the curb—no doubt with Trey behind the wheel.

The whole thing left her feeling strange, but she wasn't quite certain why. She tried to sort out her emotions. There had been plenty of them fluttering through her in the last few minutes, that was sure.

Confusion and irritation over Ginger's little temper tantrum—mixed with a healthy dose of annoyance at Dave for dating a woman like that in the first place. Then there was that flood of empathy for Caroline—though it was mixed with a bit of puzzlement about how a woman who had so much going for her could have let herself be victimized. And somehow—for reasons beyond Darcy's comprehension—she felt just a little odd because Trey had said only a casual good night to her on his way out the door.

Like you were expecting a Romeo-style farewell, she mocked herself.

"Wait a minute," she said. "How did Caroline get here? I didn't see an extra car."

Dave didn't look at her. "She called and wanted to talk to me, so I picked her up."

"I see. Chauffeur service for clients." She looked down at the still-spreading wine stain. *"It happens all the time?"* she said dryly, quoting Dave's words back at him. "Did you mean you're in the habit of cleaning up wine stains left by nervous clients, or of hiding glasses under the table to keep awkward questions at bay? Maybe from inquisitive husbands?"

His ears turned pink around the edges. "I was just trying to make Caroline feel better about the accident."

"Of course you were. Though that was probably why she was drinking the wine in the first place—to make her feel better—so overall the plan doesn't seem to have been an unmixed success."

"She seemed to need something to help her relax."

"I'd think she would," Darcy agreed. "Popping in to ask you to help her plan a party—I'm surprised a glass of wine was enough to get her over the way you must have reacted to that request. Especially that particular vintage—which I think is used more often for cooking than for drinking."

"When you actually learn to cook, Darcy, I'll take your opinions about wine more seriously. Anyway, Caroline didn't come to talk to me about the party."

"But—" Darcy waved a hand at the legal pad.

"We discussed it, yes. But that wasn't the main reason she wanted to see me." Dave dropped to one knee and began blotting at the carpet with his pocket handkerchief.

"Why did she come, then?"

"She got a call from a reporter asking why she was suddenly out of favor at Kentwells, and Trey was in."

"The Lifestyle section picking up the gossip, no doubt. You're making that stain worse, you know."

He held up his handkerchief. Once snow white, it was now brownish-red. "What was it Caroline was going to use?"

"Club soda—and no, we don't have any."

"Oh, well." Dave pushed himself up from the floor. "We'll just throw a rug over the spot."

"Shoot the moon, Dave," Darcy murmured. "Spring for new carpeting. Buy some new pocket handkerchiefs. And as long as you're going to clean house to that extent, you might consider shopping for a new girlfriend, too."

In the morning, the Kentwells store was quiet, with only a few salespeople on the floor and fewer customers in the aisles. Darcy thoughtfully considered the near-silence. It would have been a good opportunity to restock the racks, though in fact nothing seemed in need of resupplying. Perhaps, she thought, all that work had been done overnight.

Or perhaps sales were limping along and there wasn't any need to replenish the inventory. That would certainly explain why it was so important to Trey to keep this advertising campaign moving along smoothly.

Trey had been as good as his word. Darcy looked around the clothing sections for the better part of an hour without so much as a glimpse of Arabella, and when she stopped by Trey's office at the end of her shopping spree she was feeling bright and cheerful. The secretary waved her inside.

"You wanted to see me?" Darcy asked. "At least, I assumed from the frequent intercom announcements asking me to stop by the office that it must be you who was looking for me."

Trey laid a fountain pen down on his desk blotter and gestured toward her shopping bag. "You found some things you like, I see."

"It did take a while. But I even found something for you." Darcy dug to the bottom of the bag and pulled out a small, flat, gift-wrapped box.

Trey looked at it warily. "Sit down." He waved a hand toward a small couch in the corner of his office. "What did I do to deserve this?"

"It occurred to me that since you gave me an engagement gift, I should reciprocate." She flashed the amethyst ring just in case he'd let the incident slip his mind.

He sat down beside her on the couch, opened the box, and stared at the contents. "Obviously you're feeling particularly sunshiny this morning."

"It was Aunt Archie who gave me the idea," Darcy said

earnestly. "She said nobody can take themselves too seriously when they're wearing yellow socks, so I thought perhaps you would benefit from owning—"

"It's a good thing we're not keeping score when it comes to presents," Trey said. "Because an antique amethyst ring and a pair of yellow socks are nowhere near equivalent."

"*Two* pairs of socks," Darcy said. "And you're right about them not being equal, because I put a lot more thought into the socks than you did into the amethyst. Unless you're talking purely about monetary value, in which case let me point out that I don't exactly have the same level of income you do. In fact, the socks are something like the widow's mite, because that purchase did lots more damage to my budget than the amethyst did to yours."

"I'd feel more sympathetic to that argument if I wasn't going to be getting the bill for the socks sooner or later."

"I'll have you know I paid for them in cash. And unlike the amethyst, I don't expect you to return the socks when this is over."

"Very sweet of you to let me keep them as a memento. But if that's a veiled suggestion that you want to keep the amethyst—"

"As a memento, no. If you're asking whether I'm taking a page out of Aunt Archie's book so I can use it as security for my business—well, do I need to?"

"You know, Darcy, I've been thinking about that."

"My business? So have I—and I have a lot of great ideas. So if you're thinking of backing out of your commitment, don't go there, because I'm holding you to it. But all that reminds me—I'd better get ready to go earn my way out of debt on the rest of the stuff I bought this morning. I found more than I expected to." She reached for the heavy shopping bag that she'd set at her feet. "I believe Jason said we'd be looking at china today?"

"Housewares in general. Linens, china, crystal. Don't you want to know why I was paging you?"

Darcy shrugged. "I assumed you just wanted to know when I arrived—which is why I wasn't in too big a hurry to report in."

"No, I wanted to talk to you."

"Really? I'm amazed—because the way you rushed out of the cottage last night with nothing more than a muttered *See you tomorrow* left me with the impression that you didn't have much to say to me at all."

He tipped his head to one side and looked at her closely. "I understand," he said softly. "You mean you wanted more, last night."

Darcy blinked. "More what? Now wait a minute. Talk about jumping to conclusions—I was only saying that it seems odd that you want to talk to me now when you didn't have anything to say last night."

"Because I did."

There was a faint emphasis on the pronoun—so little that Darcy wasn't absolutely sure she'd heard it. She swallowed. "You want to be more specific?"

"I wanted more—last night—than a simple goodbye." His voice was low.

Darcy opened her mouth and shut it again, wondering how she had managed to so totally lose control of this conversation.

"But you're right that I didn't want to talk—exactly," Trey said. His arm curved around her shoulders, gently urging her to lean toward him.

Sitting on the deeply cushioned couch, with the shopping bag in her lap, Darcy couldn't move away.

Trey's thumb brushed her lower lip, tracing its curve, and then he kissed her, very softly and gently and slowly.

"That's why I rushed out," he said. "Because when you were kind to Caroline, I got this sudden urge to do—that."

"So this just now—it was a thank-you kiss?" Her voice felt a little ragged and she was having to focus on keeping her breathing steady. Not because the kiss had affected her, exactly, but because she was thoroughly confused. *A thank-you kiss?*

He nodded.

Okay. Whatever. And there was no reason at all, Darcy told herself firmly, to feel disappointed because that was all there was to it. Gratitude was good.

"I'm glad we got that straight," she said. "Of course it's fortunate nobody who was there last night needed to be convinced of our attachment to each other, or they'd have been left with a lot to wonder about." She pushed herself up from the couch. "See you in a few minutes. Housewares, right?"

He followed her to the door. "Wait a minute, Darcy," he said as she touched the knob. "I wasn't telling you the whole truth just now."

She turned, frowning. "Oh? Which part of what you said wasn't true?"

"The part I didn't tell you. It wasn't just you being kind to Caroline last night that made me want to kiss you."

She could suddenly feel her heartbeat, slow but almost painfully powerful, like the thump of a bass drum.

"And I didn't want to kiss you like I did just now, either. What I wanted..." He splayed his hands against the door, one on each side of her face, and bent his head.

There was nowhere for Darcy to go, and—short of hitting him with the shopping bag—not much she could do to fight him off, either. In any case, she told herself, swatting him with a loaded paper bag would leave a completely wrong impression, so the best thing to do was just let him make his point. Then she could smile and nod and get the heck out of there.

But Trey's kiss was a seduction in slow motion. The only point of contact was his lips against hers, and yet every cell of Darcy's body tingled with the impact of the slow, simple, deep kiss which paralyzed every fiber at the same time as it set off electrical shocks that made every nerve sizzle.

How—without touching anything but her lips—could he possibly make every muscle in her body feel massaged and caressed and fondled?

''That's what I wanted to do,'' he whispered against her lips.

''I see,'' Darcy managed to say. ''But you didn't do it because…?''

''Because Dave would have tried to clean my clock. Not that it's any of his business. So here's the deal, Darcy. You're an adult. I'm an adult. And if we want to lock the door and go back over to the couch…''

He was suggesting that she make love with him, right there in his office. With his secretary just outside the door and Jason pacing the floor down in the housewares department wondering where they were, Trey was suggesting that they put the world aside… He meant it, too, because if he'd been only trying to get a reaction out of her, he wouldn't have said anything about locking the door.

Darcy was stunned by the proposition. Shocked at the unexpectedness of the approach. Downright horrified at the whole idea.

Or at least, she would have been if she hadn't been thinking seriously about taking him up on it.

She caught herself just in time. What was the matter with her? She'd been through this before, and she'd made a logical, rational decision that masculine charm was never going to deceive her again. She certainly knew better than to add this sort of complication to an already-bizarre scheme. Yet with one kiss—without even a hug or a caress, for heaven's sake—he'd practically mesmerized her into going to bed with him. Did the guy put some sort of mind-altering drug in his toothpaste, or what?

She watched in a kind of daze as he reached up and loosened the knot of his tie, the same silky blue color as his eyes, and unfastened the top button of his white shirt.

He'd said once that loosening his tie was a warning of danger to come…and he'd obviously been telling the truth, even though this was an altogether different sort of danger.

Darcy ran through the first few multiplication tables in her head, just to try to clear her mind, and got hung up on three times two. "I see," she said finally. "Well, as long as we're confessing things, I must admit I didn't tell you the whole truth either, Trey."

"Really?" He sounded only vaguely interested. "Which part of what you said wasn't true?"

"The part I didn't tell you." She was deliberately quoting him. "I didn't pay full price for the socks."

"Socks?"

"Yes. You haven't forgotten the socks, have you? They were on the clearance rack and I got them for practically nothing, so the widow's mite argument doesn't really apply. Isn't it amazing, though, that no one rushed to buy two pairs of neon-yellow men's socks at full price?"

He smiled slowly. "I take it that's a no."

"You're very perceptive, Trey."

"For right now, at least."

"For—" She stopped. She'd intended to say *forever*, but somehow the word had stuck crosswise in her throat. "See you in china. The department, I mean—not the country."

She stopped outside his office, out of sight, and leaned against a wall to give a great sigh. A sigh which was merely an expression of relief, she told herself. It was certainly *not* regret over turning him down.

She ignored the little voice at the back of her mind which was calling her a liar.

It took Darcy only a minute to change into the severely plain dark red faux suede dress that she'd found hiding on a rack in the back of the sportswear department, and she was in housewares while the camera was still being set up, browsing through the china display.

But she barely saw the difference between ivory trimmed in gold and white trimmed in platinum, because she was still thinking about Trey's ludicrous proposition. What had the man been thinking of?

Wrong question, she told herself, and tried to dismiss the entire thing from her mind.

Jason bustled up to her, eyes narrowed. "What game are you playing, Darcy?"

Had he stumbled onto the truth about the engagement? That didn't exactly take the talents of Sherlock Holmes, Darcy thought—not for the man who'd been one of the engineers of the idea in the first place, and who had even worked briefly with Caroline and Corbin. The sudden change of cast and circumstances had to have looked suspicious to him. Even if Trey hadn't told him the truth, it couldn't have taken much intuition for him to guess it.

So what was she supposed to do? Treat him as a co-conspirator and confide the details, or act offended by the very suggestion that her engagement might not be all it seemed on the surface?

She opted for the middle ground. She'd play dumb and hope that Trey would show up in time to give her a cue. "I'm not sure what you mean, Jason. What game?"

"This." He pulled a sheaf of paper from his pocket,

unfolded it and thrust it at her. "Why are you applying for a job in my department?"

Darcy recognized the pages—it was part of the application package she'd so carefully assembled the night before she'd met Trey. The application package which had been mistakenly mailed because she'd forgotten all about it in the confusion. And though it wasn't specifically addressed to Jason but to the human resources director, somehow it had made it onto his desk and had been sitting there just waiting for him to stumble across it.

Jason stepped closer, looming over her. "Is this some kind of test to see what I'd do?"

"Of course not. I didn't want to push my way in, so I thought an application would be the best approach." The explanation—if it even qualified for the term—was lame, and Jason obviously knew it just as well as Darcy did, but it was too late to back out. She stumbled on. "I mean, advertising is your department, so—"

"Indeed it is. In fact, that's the only department left for me to manage—so butt out of it. I don't need your slogan suggestions, I don't need your input on how to shoot the photos and I don't need you."

"In that case," Darcy said, "I'm surprised you don't just pose a couple of mannequins instead of bothering with real people. There are plenty of them in the store, and they're experienced at standing, smiling and shutting up."

"Get changed for the shoot."

"I'm ready."

"Oh, really? Where did you get that dress?"

"Not from Arabella," she said crisply.

He glared at her.

"I take it that means you don't approve," Darcy said. "Let me count... That makes one vote in favor of the dress—mine, and one vote against—yours. I guess we need to wait and find out what Trey says."

"Trey may be the boss," Jason said through clenched teeth, "but he's not an advertising specialist."

"I may not be an ad specialist," Trey said, "but I know an appealing sight when I see one. I vote in favor. *Definitely* in favor."

Darcy turned around to see him approaching down the long aisle from luggage to housewares, passing under a metal arch which held rolled towels arranged in a full rainbow. His dark suit was a subdued spot in the prismatic color scheme, but his eyes were lit with an appreciation which glowed just as brightly as the towels.

Darcy hadn't expected quite that level of enthusiasm from him, and abruptly she wondered if the dress might be a little too figure-skimming after all. Was that what Jason had been reacting to? How would it look in the pictures, and in print? She glanced toward him, only to find that the advertising manager, jaw set as if it were stone, had walked away.

"I brought you a cappuccino," Trey said, and held out a cup. "That material your dress is made out of looks soft. May I touch it?"

"No," she said firmly, but she relaxed. This was just a continuation of what had happened in his office. Whatever had put the bee in the man's bonnet in the first place was still there. "If you must touch something, go touch a pillowcase. There are some over in the next aisle which are five hundred count Egyptian cotton."

"Is that good?"

"It must be, from the price of them. Of course I didn't comparison shop at the other end of the mall, so it's possible they're just overpriced here."

"I bet they're not as soft as your skin."

"How would you know how soft my skin is? You weren't even touching me."

He smiled. "Noticed that, did you? We could fix that oversight."

"Let's not. Look, Trey, would you cut out the flirting? What are you trying to accomplish, anyway?"

"You need an explanation?"

"No—but I'd sure like to hear a reason. The real one, preferably."

He said thoughtfully, "Maybe I should expand a bit on what I was suggesting."

"Oh, I think I got the complete picture. I just want to know what made you decide that sleeping together—with no strings, of course—would be a good idea." She sipped the cappuccino. "And by the way, I don't sleep with guys because they buy me coffee."

"That's what I was afraid you were going to say. I suppose in that case I might as well give you this, too."

She hadn't noticed that he'd still been holding one hand behind his back. In it was a bright-jacketed book of etiquette rules. She fanned the pages. "I don't think they cover this particular situation."

"How about for fun?" Trey asked.

"What?"

"Do you sleep with guys for fun?"

"Never more than one at a time."

"That's comforting."

"I mean, of course, that I never go into a bedroom with more than one guy at a time. Threesomes are just a little too tacky for me."

"Careful, you'll shock Jason."

"Oh, I'm sure he'd be delighted to have his suspicions confirmed. He really did expect to have the whole store under his command, didn't he?"

"Yes, he did."

"Well, watch out for coup attempts. Maybe he's the one who tipped off the reporter."

Trey's eyebrows went up slightly. "I didn't tell you about the reporter."

"No, you didn't. Dave did. He told me there was a reporter after Caroline yesterday."

"I wonder what happened to client privilege."

"Maybe he thought the guy might pop up wanting to talk to me next, and I should be warned," Darcy said coolly.

"I intended to tell you about it—and that I've handled the situation already. In fact, that's why I paged you this morning, but then you distracted me."

"*I* distracted *you?*"

"The yellow socks," he reminded.

"Hand them over—I'll take them back."

"You can't if they were on final clearance."

"I didn't say I wanted my money back. But if that's going to keep you from telling me things I need to know—"

"Like the reporter?"

"That's the first thing that comes to mind, but not the only one. I'd kind of like to know what's going to happen at this engagement party. Were you actually serious about inviting the competition? And if you have any more Aunt Archies lurking in the family tree. And when we're going to start working seriously on this business of mine. And—"

"Jason's ready to shoot. We'll talk about it over dinner."

"What if I already have plans?"

"You don't. I'm the only guy in your life right now. Besides, I still have to explain to you why I think it's a good idea to sleep together. Or would you rather I tell you right now, between photographs?"

CHAPTER SEVEN

BAITING her might not be very smart, Trey admitted, but it certainly was entertaining. It also had the side benefit of distracting her from bringing up topics which might tempt Jason to start asking uncomfortable questions, if he happened to overhear a chance word.

Darcy smiled at him. "Tell me right now," she suggested. "Because I'm sure the crew would be agog to find out that we're not already sleeping together."

She really was delightful, calling his bluff like that. "You're making my argument for me, you know. As long as you're pointing out how silly it is not to share a bed, I don't even have to try to be convincing."

"That wasn't what I said. Anyway, save it for someone who's interested, Trey."

"Oh, you're interested, all right." He stretched out a hand to cup her cheek.

Darcy reached up to the archway and pulled a rolled towel out of the rainbow.

From the corner of his eye, Trey saw a streak of yellow descending toward his face as she gave the towel an expert flip, cracking it like a whip. "Hey," he protested. "Easy on the merchandise."

"I'll buy it as a souvenir."

"I can think of more memorable ones." He pulled it away from her and draped the terry cloth over her head. "That's not your best color, you know."

"Watch the hair," she ordered and blindly pulled down two more towels, one with each hand, waving them as if she were taunting a bull.

"The heck with your hair. I like it better tousled anyway."

"If all of you are ready to stop being juvenile," Jason said, "let's get to work."

The crew had been grinning, but Trey noted that the smiles suddenly died under the lash of Jason's voice.

Obviously Darcy was feeling reluctant to settle to the task, for she took her time rolling up the towels once more. Then she stood on her toes, trying to fit them back into the metal rings which formed the rainbow arch.

Trey watched with patient interest, intrigued by the softly rounded curves of her lithe body as she reached as far as she could above her head. Though she'd been just exactly tall enough to pull the towels down, it seemed she lacked a couple of inches of being able to put them back into place.

Finally she turned to him. "Would you help me with this?"

"In return for that smile—yes, of course."

She held out the towels, but instead of taking them to put back in place, Trey reached for her instead. With his hands on her waist, he lifted her toward the arch.

She gave a little shriek and for a moment he thought she was going to overbalance them both. Then she clutched the support of the archway, put the towels back so they looked almost the same as before she'd started yanking at them and looked down at him. "I'm finished. You can put me down now. And warn me next time."

"I did warn you," Trey said. He set her down, but he let his hands linger at her waist. "I said I wanted to touch your dress—and this seemed as good a way as any."

For Darcy, the day was both longer and even more difficult than the previous one had been. Jason seemed even more driven, as though her insistence on choosing her own clothes—and then Trey backing up her opinion—had undercut his authority with his crew. He seemed to be determined to get his standing back, even if he had to do it by force.

Maybe it would have been easier just to go along with Arabella's choices, Darcy thought. Besides, if she'd been wearing polyester rather than faux suede, then maybe Trey wouldn't be seizing any excuse to put a guiding hand on her sleeve or brush an imaginary speck of lint off her shoulder...

On the other hand, it might not make any difference. The suede dress had made a handy excuse, but she suspected that even if she'd been wearing feathers and he was allergic to them, Trey would be hanging on to her arm and explaining that he had to keep a hold on her because his eyes were watering too badly to see. He'd do whatever it took to keep her off balance.

Because it was apparent to Darcy that *off balance* was exactly where he wanted to keep her. What was really infuriating was that recognizing the strategy didn't help at all to get her feet solidly on the ground once more.

Every time she glanced his way, even when he wasn't touching her, she could once again feel again the warmth of his hands on her waist as he'd lifted her as effortlessly and gracefully as if she were a ballerina. When she did manage to stop thinking for a moment about the way he'd held her, she found herself watching his lips and feeling once more the softly insistent pressure of his mouth against hers.

And then, when she was able to force her thoughts away from the kiss, she couldn't help remembering how easily he'd let her go there in his office, when she'd changed the subject and made it clear she wasn't going to join him in a quick tryst on the couch. He'd yielded with a smile and a quick remark which indicated more humor than disappointment, followed up by a continual program of teasing…

He might have been serious about locking the door and making love to her. She suspected he wouldn't have been at all reluctant to enjoy the interlude. But it clearly hadn't been passion he'd been feeling so much as mere curiosity, or he wouldn't have given up so easily when she'd hesitated.

And what about you, Darcy? What are you feeling?

She hadn't expected that question to come up, not where Trey was concerned. This was a business proposition, pure and simple, and feelings shouldn't have come into it at all. But now that the line had been crossed between business and emotion…she had to admit she wasn't quite sure what she was feeling. She was irritated at him for taking advantage of the situation, that was for sure. Intrigued by what on earth his reasons could be. Fascinated by what he might be plotting. Annoyed at…

Jason swore. "Come on, Darcy, stop looking sour and get with the program."

She pulled herself together. *Not now,* she thought. Later, she'd have time just to sit still and think.

Time was what she needed, to sort everything out in her head and decide what to do. Time to think about the situation, and about what she wanted, and about Trey.

Especially about Trey, a little voice whispered in the back of her brain.

Darcy did her best to ignore it.

When the final photographs of the day were done, Darcy felt like flopping onto the nearest horizontal surface to take a nap. However, since every flat surface in sight was metal and most of them were pieces of refrigerators, washing machines and microwaves, she thought better of the idea.

"I need to check in with Carol and tie up the loose ends

of the day," Trey said with a glance at his wristwatch. "See what's been going on while I've been stuck here. Do you want to come up to the office with me, or shop?"

Darcy tried without much success to stifle a groan, and she punched him lightly in the arm. "After a day like this, you can not only suggest shopping but keep a straight face while you say the words? You must be a heck of a poker player."

"What we've been doing all day isn't shopping," Trey pointed out.

"No, but it's close enough to the reality that the whole idea is painful. Fingering fabrics, asking pointed questions, actually thinking about colors...."

"I thought women could always shop."

"Only if it's also a social occasion. You know, like with girlfriends. I'm going home."

"Dinner," he said succinctly. "Remember? We're going to talk about all those questions which you said earlier were on your mind—but which I can't remember just now."

"Well, conveniently for you, I'm not hungry and I'm too tired to talk. Right now all I want is to get out of these—"

Trey's eyes brightened. "Clothes?"

Darcy didn't miss a beat. "*Shoes* and get comfortable."

He glanced down at her feet. "You're the one who chose those shoes."

"Yes. That doesn't prevent them from being a mistake." She started toward the door.

"Okay, go home and get comfortable. I'll pick up something and come by the cottage."

"I just said no."

"You have to eat to keep up your strength. You want Mexican? Thai? Polynesian? Italian?"

"Martian would be good," Darcy mused. "Of course, the nearest drive-through might be a little out of the way, so feel free to give up the idea entirely. See you tomorrow.''

She looked around for her shopping bag and spotted it just beyond the pile of camera equipment. The art director, supervising the equipment breakdown, handed it to her. ''The best thing we shot all day was the stunt with the towels,'' he said.

''I don't doubt it.''

''Jason won't agree, of course. It's too bad.''

Darcy smiled. She liked the young man and admired the way he managed to work with his boss despite Jason's difficulties. ''If he thought using those pictures would embarrass me, he'd probably run with them.'' She waved the bag and headed for the parking lot. Even the huge bunches of balloons outside the Tyler-Royale store at the far end of the mall didn't inspire her to go look.

I may never enjoy shopping again, she thought. Though that might not be such a bad thing, because it would certainly be easier on the budget.

Traffic was atrocious. While the delays at every red light wore on her nerves, there was a positive side as well, Darcy told herself. By the time she got to the cottage, Dave's office hours would be over, he and Mrs. Cusack would both be gone and she wouldn't have to deal with inane questions about her day. She hoped.

Once into the quieter neighborhood where the cottage nestled, her luck changed—cars seemed to speed out of her way, there was an empty parking spot right in front, the lights were off, and the discreet Closed sign was in place. Looking forward to blessed silence and a tall glass of cranberry juice mixed with sparkling water, Darcy unlocked the front door, pushed it open and stopped dead on the threshold.

The reception room looked as if it were a dollhouse which had been tipped over by a careless child, then set upright again without any attempt to put the furniture back into place. Mrs. Cusack's desk, the couch and clients' chairs, file cabinets, coffee table—all had been shoved around the corner into the nook which led to the kitchen. The old carpet and underlying padding were gone, and scattered on the bare, rough plywood of the floor were a carpentry shop's worth of tools, several gallon cans of glue, and dozens of open boxes of boards—a new, already-stained, polished and elegant wood floor. Or, rather, a few thousand pieces of wood and the necessary equipment and supplies to someday make them fit into a new floor.

Spring for new carpeting, she'd told Dave last night. It sounded as if he'd taken her seriously for once. But why did it have to be today?

All Darcy wanted was to collapse. But the couch had been shoved up against a row of filing cabinets and piled full of the detritus of the reception room—a couple of wastebaskets, the paper shredder, a silk ficus tree, a lamp. Mrs. Cusack's desk—looking even bigger than usual in the small nook—was blocking the stairway to the penthouse as securely as if it were a bank vault.

There was no place to sit, and she couldn't get upstairs for a change of clothes or even a different pair of shoes. For all practical purposes, Darcy's possessions had been pared down to what was on her back or in the shopping bag she carried.

She pulled out her cell phone to call Dave. But he didn't answer. Instead his phone kicked back over to the office number, giving her a polite voice mail message that his office would be closed on Friday for remodeling.

"I gathered that much already," Darcy muttered and hung up. There was no point in leaving a message on the office machine when she was the only one there to hear it. "Dammit, Dave, why did you have to get organized over *this?* The one time in your life when I wish you'd procrastinate—but no, today you have to be right on top of things. It's not like there weren't already stains on that carpet. Nobody would have noticed one more for a few weeks—or even months.''

The front door creaked open. ''Talking to yourself again?''

Darcy spun around.

Trey, carrying a shopping bag which was a match for her own, pushed the door shut behind him. ''You shouldn't leave this unlocked when you're here alone, you know. Anybody could walk in.''

''Whether they've been invited or not,'' Darcy pointed out. ''And as long as we're on the subject, I don't remember inviting you.''

''Oh, that's all right—I knew what you meant. You clearly indicated that you'd like Martian for dinner, so I took it as an invitation.''

''I didn't mean it that way. Still, I must say I'm glad to see you after all.''

Trey kept on talking. ''So I brought you Martian. Actually I brought the closest approximation I could find.''

It hadn't taken him very long. Darcy was curious despite herself. ''And that would be?''

He looked around as if seeing the mess in the room for the first time. ''Is there a place to set down the bag?''

''If you mean somewhere that's flat and empty, probably not within three blocks.''

''I suppose we could use the boxes of wood as a picnic table.''

''Oh, why not? I'm sure Dave wouldn't mind.''

Trey stacked up a half-dozen boxes to form a makeshift table, sat down on a gallon glue bucket and began removing containers from the shopping bag. ''I'm a little surprised,'' he said, and tapped a fingertip on the glossy surface of the top board in the package.

"By the quick action to replace the floor? I am, too. Maybe the stain was worse than I thought—I didn't really look at it this morning." Darcy took her own seat on a matching glue can, sitting carefully in order to keep her hemline somewhere near normal. Trey's gaze flickered toward her knees, and she was glad she'd made the extra effort. "Dave's usual pattern would be to get around to calling a carpet place about next February, picking a new pattern by July and having it installed by the following Christmas."

"I know. But I was talking about the hardwood. It's not exactly the best budget alternative."

"It was hard to move furniture on the carpet, so I guess he thought a hard surface would be better even if it cost more to start with."

"You mean *that* furniture?" He waved a hand toward Mrs. Cusack's desk. "It's going to be hard to move anywhere, anytime. That desk is the size of an aircraft carrier."

"Yes, Dave bought it at an auction intending to use it back in his office, but it wouldn't fit around the corner and through the door."

"And he couldn't figure that out while the bidding was still going on? Good thing he decided on law as a profession instead of math."

"He did almost flunk geometry."

"No joke." Trey handed her a foam container and a spoon. "You don't suppose he's planning to put this floor down himself, do you?"

"Dave?" Darcy stared at him in horror, and only when she looked again at the tools did she begin to breathe once more. "No. Those saws and things belong to somebody who knows what he's doing. Not a novice."

"That's good. I don't need my lawyer cutting off his arm right now."

Darcy took the lid off the container he'd given her and

looked doubtfully at the contents. "Okay, I'll bite. What made you decide split pea soup is Martian?"

He grinned. "I'm glad you asked. If we are what we eat, then surely the little green men on Mars are, too. So—"

Darcy rolled her eyes. "I suppose you've got a spinach salad in there as well?"

"Yes, and celery, broccoli and asparagus spears with guacamole dip. But not everything I brought is green. We have hard rolls—because they looked sort of like the boulders on Mars. And chocolate for dessert because it's universal." Trey popped the top of his own container of soup and dug in. "What are you going to wear to the engagement party?"

"I hadn't decided. In fact, I was still hoping to cancel the whole thing."

"Not a chance. There was a message from Caroline in my stack this afternoon—she's invited a hundred and fifty people, she's hired two bands so there will be a choice of dance music, and she wanted to know whether there was anything in the way of food which you preferred not to serve. I told her you'd call her back."

"Sounds like she's doing just fine on her own. Two bands?"

"A string quartet for Aunt Archie's music room, a rock and roll group for the terrace."

"She couldn't get by with a disc jockey who could do both?"

"Caroline? You're joking. She never does anything halfway." He looked thoughtfully at the bare floor. "Which I suppose explains the hardwood, too."

"You mean because it was her wineglass I kicked, she's replacing the floor altogether? It would have been adequate to send over a carpet cleaning service and give me half the bill. Your sister's got an overactive conscience, you know—that's probably why she let Corbin push her around."

"To say nothing of the problem it leaves for you," Trey mused. "Unless you plan to saw a hole in the wall, I don't see how you're going to get upstairs."

Darcy gave him her most winning smile. "I did say I was glad to see you," she reminded. "I was sort of hoping you'd give the desk a shove so I could get to the door."

Trey didn't even glance at it. "Not me. I have a sore shoulder from somebody punching me in the arm when I suggested she go shopping."

"Come on, Trey. You'd just picked me up bodily, so I doubt that little tap on the arm caused you any pain."

Trey snapped his fingers. "I'd forgotten that—the gymnastics stunt must be why my shoulder is sore."

"What a gentleman you are," she said sweetly, "to imply that lifting me is harder than bench-pressing weights."

"It's because you wriggle—the weights don't. Come to think of it, both my shoulders are sore. That confirms it—no furniture moving for me, today. So what are you going to do?"

Darcy hadn't wanted to even think about it. Now he was leaving her no choice but to consider her options. She took another bite of her soup. "I tried calling Dave to see if I can crash at his place, but he's not answering his cell phone. There's a spare key to his apartment in the bottom drawer of Mrs. Cusack's desk, but—"

Trey looked over his shoulder. "That would be the drawer that's pushed up tight against the stairway door?"

"That's the one. In any case, even if I could get to the key, I wouldn't want to walk into his apartment without warning."

"You mean in case he's entertaining Ginger? I doubt he will be. She seemed to think he owed her a very large apology, so it's more likely to be roses, jewelry and a lavish dinner out."

"Still, if there's the faintest chance he'll be bringing her home with him, I don't want to be anywhere around," Darcy said.

"I can't argue with you there."

"And I don't want to be a nuisance to anyone, so I suppose that really only leaves one choice."

"I agree," Trey said easily. "It's settled, then. You're coming home with me."

Darcy said, for at least the fifth time, "I meant I'd go to a hotel tonight." She was beginning to feel cranky. She'd finished her soup and salad and was starting to think that pelting Trey with hard rolls might get his attention. It was a dead certainty that nothing else was going to do it.

"It could take days to get all that flooring laid," he pointed out.

"Dave's voice mail says the office will be closed on Friday, that's all."

"But it's always closed on weekends, so he wouldn't make a point of telling clients that anyway."

She had to admit he was right about that much. And the stack of materials looked like much more than one day's worth of work.

"And even when the floor's down," Trey went on, "it can't be walked on for a while. I'm guessing you'll be out of the penthouse till sometime next week."

"All right," Darcy said. "I give up. I admit I need a place to stay for a few days. But not with you. I'm supposed to call Caroline anyway, so maybe she'll take me in."

Trey shook his head. "Not unless you want to sleep standing up in her closet. Why do you think she's throwing this bash at Aunt Archie's, anyway?"

"Aunt Archie," Darcy said triumphantly. "I bet she has scads of extra bedrooms."

"Yes, plus she has a very big bump of curiosity about what's going on, and no tact whatsoever."

Darcy chewed her lip. "I'm not sleeping with you," she said firmly.

Trey grinned.

Darcy felt hot color spurt through her face. "And I didn't mean I'd be staying awake with you, either!"

"Sweetheart, that's such a wide-open line that I'd be ashamed of myself for taking the bait. I do have standards, you know. Besides," he added prosaically, "there are so many snappy comebacks I'll have to think about which one would be most devastating to your defenses."

"I'll be holding my breath while I wait," she muttered.

"If you're finished with the asparagus, I'll start picking things up. Where do you want the leftovers?"

"Considering we can't get into the kitchen to put them in the refrigerator, I guess we throw everything out. There's a garbage can in—" She stopped.

"—in the kitchen, I know. All right, I'll gather up the remainders to take with us, while you get your stuff."

"What stuff?" she asked morosely.

He grinned at her. "Whatever stuff you can get together," he said gently. "Because I only loan my toothbrush to girls who are sleeping with me."

Trey's apartment was near the top of one of Chicago's most exclusive and expensive bits of real estate, occupying— Darcy estimated—half of an entire floor. From the uncurtained windows of the big living room, Darcy could look south over a golden net of city lights which seemed to stretch forever, or east to the blackness of Lake Michigan.

"Make yourself at home," Trey said. "There's never much in the kitchen, but there's a deli downstairs that does takeout, and I've heard rumors about a supermarket that delivers."

"Rumors? You don't know the easiest way to get a gallon of milk?"

"Why would I want a gallon of milk? I don't take baths in the stuff. Speaking of which, the timer's broken on the whirlpool tub in the master bathroom. No matter how long you set it for, it turns off in ten minutes. It's very disruptive."

"I imagine it would be," Darcy agreed idly. "But that's all right, because I don't expect to have any reason to go into the master bathroom." She turned away from the window. If she was going to be here for several days, there would be another opportunity to enjoy the view.

Trey was already halfway down the hall. "But of course you will," he called over his shoulder. "This way."

Darcy froze in midstep, but he was too far away to shout after him, so she followed. "What do you mean?" she asked suspiciously. "Because if you're going to tell me a place like this only has one bathroom—or one bedroom—"

"No, there are two. And like the good host I am, I'm giving you the preferred quarters—master suite, with attached bath, rather than the guest room with the cot."

"The cot would be fine. I'm used to a futon."

Trey shook his head. "A futon? Then you definitely need your beauty sleep. Besides, if I put you in the guest room, you'd be yelling at me for leering at you as you cross the hall in your dressing gown to get in the shower."

"You could just not leer," Darcy pointed out, "and then there wouldn't be a problem."

Trey's gaze flickered down the length of her body and then back up. "I could try." His very tone oozed doubt, and Darcy gave it up.

"This isn't a bad idea, anyway," Trey said. "If you're going to be choosing linens for the place, perhaps you should know what it looks like."

She eyed him suspiciously. "You're absolutely certain it was Caroline's idea to replace the floor this weekend?"

"Darling, surely you're not implying that I might have manipulated the situation."

"Will you swear you didn't?"

"No," Trey said cheerfully. "Because I would have manipulated it—I just didn't happen to think of it. It's all those photographic flashes, I suppose. Or else it's you. Yes, now that I think about it, definitely you're the reason my brain's turning to mush."

That would be extremely scary, Darcy thought, if it were true. But of course it wasn't—it was simply another flirtatious way to keep her guessing.

Someday, she thought, some woman would actually manage to turn Trey Kent's brain to mush. Darcy just hoped she wouldn't be there to see the show—it would just be too painful to see the man who always had an answer, who was always three steps ahead, acting like a lovestruck fool. Especially if the woman in question didn't deserve him.

She pushed the thought away and followed him into the master suite. The bedroom was huge, facing west over the city, and here the golden net of city lights spread even more thickly, stretching as far as she could see. "No curtains here, either?" she asked.

"On the sixty-fourth floor, who's going to be looking in?"

He had a point, Darcy admitted. Window-washers perhaps. Hang-gliders caught in the currents off the lake. Circus people who were shot out of cannons… "How long have you lived here?"

"Just since my father got sick and I came home."

"You never told me where you lived before that."

"You never asked. I was in Philadelphia. The cleaning staff was here today, so the sheets and towels are fresh. If there's anything you need…'' He grinned. ''Like, for instance, the loan of a toothbrush…''

''I'll deal with it, thanks. And you'll be the first person I call if I get lonely. Just don't let the hope keep you awake.''

He murmured something that she was pretty sure *wasn't* a good night, and closed the bedroom door behind him.

Darcy didn't expect to sleep at all. It would have been difficult enough to rest in the guest room, with only a wall between them. But here, in his king-sized bed, with the pillows he regularly used and the scent of his aftershave lingering in the air…how was she supposed to ignore all that?

But the mattress welcomed her tired muscles like the embrace of a lover, the pillow caressed her cheek and the aftershave was like the relaxing scent of herbs drifting on a soft breeze. Before she could even nestle into her favorite sleeping position, she'd dropped off.

The scent of coffee woke her. Not the overbrewed, acid smell of Dave's coffee, but a fresh, inviting aroma that lifted her head off the pillow to sniff.

Trey was lounging on the bed beside her, clad in baggy sweatpants and nothing else, holding a cup under her nose. ''Well, that's two more facts I know about you now,'' he said. ''Coffee is the only thing that gets your attention first thing in the morning, and you snore.''

''I do not.''

''How would you know? You were asleep. And your voice sounds sexy as hell when you first wake up. That makes three facts. Keep going, this is interesting.''

Darcy propped herself up higher and took the coffee mug out of his hand. The mug was chipped and stained, and on the side was blazoned *Lions do it with pride.* She took a long swallow of the coffee and felt warmth and energy spread through her veins. ''Trey, is there any feminine voice that *doesn't* sound sexy as hell to you in the morning?"

He considered. "Caroline's. And Aunt Archie's."

"I rest my case."

"Want a bagel? I'll call down to the deli and have them send some up."

"I assumed you'd already called the deli. You made the coffee yourself?"

"It's my one talent in the kitchen."

"Don't make light of it." She took another long, contemplative swallow. "For this, I just might keep you after all."

His voice was lazy. "Don't threaten me like that."

The quick reaction confirmed Darcy's convictions that he hadn't turned to mush, no matter what he'd said last night. *And you're pleased,* she reminded herself. *So make it clear that you don't take him seriously; tease him right back.* "Hey, don't they say that possession is nine-tenths of the law? Now that I've moved in…"

He leaned closer and whispered, "So possess me, Darcy."

She shifted uneasily away. "Um…I—"

"And that's fact number four—you can obviously talk in your sleep even after you've started drinking your coffee. Now that you're finally awake, do you want part of the newspaper?" He reached onto the floor and tossed the morning's paper onto her lap, deftly extracting the sports section as it fell. He leaned back against the pillows, set his mug on the taut muscles of his stomach and scanned the headlines.

"You're going to sit here in bed and read the paper?"

"Unless you're offering me some better way to greet the day. Your photo debut is in the lifestyle section, by the way."

"The first ad?" She shot up straight, almost dislodging

his mug from its perch on his abdominal muscles, just as the phone rang on the night table beside her. She glanced at the display panel and felt like swearing. "The message says it's Caroline calling. I'll just be very quiet, and she'll never know I'm here, okay?"

Trey reached across her to snag the phone. "Hey, Caroline," he said. "How's the weather down there?"

Darcy couldn't stop herself. "Down where?" she breathed.

"Down on the fortieth floor, where her apartment is," Trey said. "What, Caroline? Oh, that was just Darcy asking where you were. We're drinking coffee and reading the paper, trying to decide whether to get up or just pull the covers over our heads again and—" He turned the phone a fraction of an inch away from his mouth and looked curiously at Darcy. "Why are you making noises like a tea-kettle? I thought you said you were going to be quiet so Caroline wouldn't know you're here."

CHAPTER EIGHT

TREY propped the phone between his shoulder and his ear, so he could hear Caroline, drink coffee and turn the pages of the sports section all at once. But in fact his attention wasn't on any of the three things—he was watching Darcy from the corner of his eye. She not only sounded like a teakettle with the lid on too tight, making soft hissing noises that threatened to explode at any instant, but she appeared to be just as hot as one, too.

"What was that again, Caroline?" he asked. "Oh, right—the food. Where did you find a caterer who'd let you make menu changes the day before the party, anyway? Never mind. Do you want to talk to Darcy about it?"

He looked over the edge of the paper, but Darcy was shaking her head. "Any kind of food is okay with me," she said.

"Anything goes except sushi. No, that's not Darcy's order, it's mine. And an absolute minimum of alfalfa sprouts and tofu, too. Look, we need to get going, or Jason will be having a fit…. Okay, see you tomorrow night." He put the phone down and folded the newspaper. "When you hiss like that, Darcy, you sound like a rattlesnake in heat."

"Funny that particular reptile should be the one to come to your mind," she snapped. "All right, I admit I should have kept my mouth shut like I said I was going to. But you didn't have to paint her a billboard!"

Trey shrugged. "She has a sixth sense about these things."

"And how did she develop it, I wonder? From having a lot of experience at calling you up and finding you in bed with a woman?"

"What's the matter with you? It's only Caroline, for heaven's sake. She's not going to take it seriously."

"Serious or not, we don't need to convince Caroline we're sleeping together. In fact, it's a really bad idea for Caroline to get the notion that we're sleeping together. And I'd also appreciate you not making me sound just like all the other women you know."

"Trust me, Darcy, you're not anywhere near in the same category as the other women I know."

"Thanks." The word sounded as if she'd clipped it off with a pair of garden shears.

What the hell? First she didn't want to be like the other women he knew, and then she did? "Dammit, I meant that as a compliment."

"Yes, of course you did."

"Remember? I didn't want to end up engaged to any of them, even temporarily."

"Because they *would* be trying to convince Caroline there was something more serious than just being caught in bed together?"

He hesitated, not quite sure of the answer she expected. He was beginning to think there were no safe replies where Darcy Malone was concerned. "Right."

Not that any of the beauties in question would have actually been in his bed this morning, he thought. Maybe some other time, and for all the usual reasons—but definitely not under these circumstances. For most of them, he'd have happily moved the equivalent of Mrs. Cusack's desk so they could get to their usual quarters.

Whoa, Kent. So why did you refuse to move it so Darcy could?

Because he didn't much like the idea of her living in that attic in the first place, all alone in what wasn't exactly the best neighborhood in town. Besides, Darcy was different. And there was no reason for either of them to hit the panic button about that. The very fact that she was here this morning—that he'd invited her to spend the night in his bed—was all the evidence she should need to realize that he respected all the things that made her unlike the others.

None of that meant that he didn't want to sleep with her—because he did. And if anything, that was the final proof that he didn't regard her in the same light as the other women he knew. There wasn't a one of them he'd trust not to get the wrong idea if he climbed under the covers. But Darcy—Darcy was safe. She'd said herself that she was every bit as skittish as he was where permanent commitments were concerned.

Now if he could just figure out how to explain the fine points of his reasoning to her, so she'd get off his back about it... Not likely, he decided. He might as well give it up and go with the flow.

"Well," Darcy said, "you'd better be more worried about Dave than about Caroline."

He was barely listening. "My good pal Dave?"

"My big brother Dave," Darcy emphasized. "Because he's probably going to invite you into the alley for a brawl."

"I doubt it. I'm one of his better-paying clients."

"But if Caroline tells him about finding us in bed together—"

"She didn't exactly find us, so why would she go running to Dave about it? And even if she did, why would he get upset?"

"You seemed to think yesterday that he'd have something to say about it."

"No, I just said I wasn't going to do anything right in front of him. Anyway, he knows there's nothing serious going on here."

"Great. It feels so much better to know that my brother will be thinking of me as a slut for going to bed with someone I don't even care about."

"If you like, I'll call Dave and reassure him that we're not sleeping together."

She sounded doubtful. "You'd do that? Thanks—I think."

"Of course I will," Trey assured her. "I'll be happy to tell him there was no sleeping going on at all."

She took a swing at him. It went wild, of course, but it gave Trey all the excuse he needed. He grabbed her wrist and pulled, and since she was already off balance it took very little force to drag her across the bed till she was lying half across him, her face very close to his, the scent of her shampoo teasing his nose as her hair fell around his face, and her breasts soft and warm against his bare chest, with the T-shirt he'd loaned her to sleep in separating his skin from hers. "Hi," he said softly. "The penalty for hitting is that you have to forfeit a kiss."

"And the penalty for yanking and shoving is that you get bitten." She planted a hand on his chest and pushed herself up.

"Biting?" Trey shook his head sadly. "Darcy, you really shouldn't make promises you don't intend to keep."

In any case, he thought, the real penalty for what he'd done wasn't anything she could threaten—it was that he'd found himself in a very intimate position with a woman who had no intention of letting things go any further.

And a rotten shame that was, too.

They were late, of course, and Jason was pacing the floor by the cosmetics counter near the door, where Justine was waiting with her bottles and jars and tubes already laid out. Darcy pulled off her jacket and settled in to let Justine do her makeup.

"How did you like the first ad?" the woman asked as she began smoothing moisturizer into Darcy's face.

Only then did Darcy remember the newspaper she'd been paging through when the telephone rang. In her irritation at Trey, she'd forgotten all about the ad. "I haven't seen it yet," she admitted.

"We were too busy this morning," Trey said with a smile. "Want some breakfast, sweetheart? You really shouldn't go into the day without eating. I'll get you something from the coffee shop while Justine's working you over."

Justine choked back a giggle, and Darcy briefly considered grabbing the nearest squirt bottle and using it on Trey in lieu of pepper spray. "No, thanks, darling."

"The ad came out reasonably well," Jason said, "considering the rush we were in to get the pieces together. The next one will be better. Now that I know you're both here, I'll be up in housewares. We'll start off the morning with china."

"I thought you were doing china yesterday," Justine said.

Darcy obediently tipped her head back so Justine could apply foundation. "We didn't get to it."

"Because you were too busy playing with towels," Jason said over his shoulder.

Darcy waited till he was out of earshot and Trey's cheerful whistle had died away in the direction of the coffee shop. "You wouldn't happen to have a copy of that ad handy, would you, Justine?"

"Sure thing." Her hands still covered with foundation, Justine reached under the counter and picked the newspaper page up with the tips of her nails.

Darcy took one look and sighed. "I knew as soon as Jason said he liked it that I'd come off looking like the dowdy stepsister. The ring really shows up nicely, though."

"And the kiss photo is good," Justine allowed. "Though it needs to be lots bigger to be really effective. The art director and I were talking about that right before you came in. He said the two pictures are actually backward."

"Backward?"

"He says the kiss should be huge to get attention, and the merchandise should be small, like it's an afterthought."

Darcy nodded. "I've had enough advertising experience to know he's right."

That was one point in Jason's favor, however. As long as he was in charge, she wouldn't be splashed over the newspaper pages kissing Trey in larger-than-life size. Which just went to show that there was always something to be grateful for.

She had to walk almost past jewelry to get to china, and she purposely detoured into the department to tell the manager how beautiful her amethyst had looked in the ad. She didn't realize until she was inside that Trey was already there, leaning over the counter and studying a sheet of paper which lay in front of him.

"Good morning, Ms. Malone." Deftly the manager slid the paper out of the way. It was a sketch—Darcy could see the shape of a ring, with some kind of stones drawn in, but she couldn't make out the details.

Trey turned around. "I was on my way to get you a bagel," he said, "because all you had this morning was coffee. You can't expend energy at the rate you do and not eat."

Darcy saw the manager grin. Trying to stop Trey was futile, she knew, so she decided to ignore him. "Is that my ring you were looking at?"

"You're wearing your ring."

"No, my..." She paused. "My other ring." She couldn't bring herself to say *my wedding ring;* since there wouldn't be a wedding, there would never be a need for a ring to seal the marriage vows. It was just part of the image.

"It's only a sketch," Trey said. "It might not end up looking anything like this."

No doubt that was true, she thought. He'd probably already put all sorts of changes and conditions on the sketch, just to delay the work. The longer it took to get a sketch he approved, the more likely that the engagement would be officially finished before the jewelers ever started to make the ring.

And the fact that there probably wouldn't ever be a ring at all was no doubt why she was so eager to look at the sketch—because something deep inside her wanted to know what it might have looked like.

"Exactly," Darcy said. "Don't you think I should have a say about it, while there's still time to modify the design? You said I should choose the engagement ring I wanted, since I was the one who would be wearing it. The same thing should be true of—" She stopped again, unwilling to say the words.

Trey shrugged. "Show her."

The manager pulled the sheet of paper out once more.

She'd caught only a glimpse of the sketch before, but now she could see that it was actually a finished drawing, finely detailed and lovingly shaded. The design wasn't a single ring but a double one—two bands, each only slightly narrower than the engagement ring, fitting on either side of the big amethyst. She sent a quizzical look at the manager.

"We call it a jacket," he said eagerly. "Most wedding sets are designed together, so the wedding ring fits very naturally around the setting of the stone in the engagement ring. But when we start with a ring which was intended to be worn alone, it's a little more difficult. The whole thing looks odd if we just add an extra band."

She looked at the amethyst on her hand and realized he was right; fitting a band around one end of the stone would be awkward and the result would look makeshift because it had been cobbled together.

"So we design a whole new package," the manager went on. "We build on what we have to bring everything into balance."

There was no question he'd accomplished that, Darcy

thought. The finished setting was perfectly coordinated; the jacket was as large as the original ring, and each section of it was crusted with a row of smaller amethysts to pick up the color of the main stone. The overall effect was awe-inspiring. It was also massive—her finger would be paved with amethysts all the way to the first knuckle.

"It's beautiful," she said, sincerely. "But it's not me."

The manager looked too stunned to answer.

Darcy added hastily, "It's—well, it's a little heavy on the purple, for one thing. Don't you think?"

Trey asked, "What would you suggest?"

His tone was idle, only mildly interested, and Darcy shot him a warning look. If he was so anxious for everyone in the store to get the idea that they hadn't bothered with breakfast because they were too busy making love, surely he could make a little effort to help the jewelry manager believe that he actually cared what she thought about a wedding ring.

But he didn't seem to notice her glare, so Darcy turned to the manager instead. "I think the double row of amethysts overwhelms the engagement ring," she said. "But if you were to make the band on each side thinner, and rather than covering it with stones, just put a diamond chip on each side of the main stone…" She slipped a pen from Trey's shirt pocket, flipped over the paper and began to sketch. "Here. Like this."

The manager stared at her with brows raised.

Too late, Darcy realized that it might not be very smart to tell a professional what was wrong with his design, or how to fix it. And that drawing had been the work of an artist who clearly loved his subject. While she…

She knew what she was talking about when it came to her own taste, but that didn't exactly make her an expert on jewelry design. Skill with a pencil didn't translate into an eye for craftsmanship, and she knew it. Yet she'd plunged right in and dictated what he should do.

"It's just an idea," she said lamely.

The manager transferred his gaze to Trey, but his eyebrows remained in the upright position.

Trey said, as if he were apologizing, "Well, she is a graphic artist."

Darcy wanted to stamp on his foot. "I'm sorry," she said. "I didn't mean to cause trouble." She turned on her heel and started toward the main aisle.

Trey said something to the manager—a few words that she didn't catch—and caught up with her within a few strides. "Don't go all stiff and proper about it. He wasn't offended at your suggestions."

"You could have fooled me."

"I mean it. It was a good idea—much nicer than the purple monster he'd designed."

She smiled despite herself. *Purple monster* was a pretty good way to describe the ring in that drawing. "And it would be a lot less expensive, too, with a couple of diamond chips instead of twenty or thirty little amethysts."

"That's true," Trey said. "He'll draw it up again."

"I'm glad I could help you with the delaying process." She paused at the edge of the housewares department. "Before we go in to look at china, is there anything we should talk about? I mean, if one of us likes plain and simple and the other's into Hawaiian flowers, maybe we should decide right now—" She stopped. "Is that Caroline?"

"Where?"

"What do you mean, where? Over there, under the sombrero, wearing the dark glasses."

It wasn't actually a sombrero, Darcy decided on second glance, just a straw hat with the widest brim she had ever seen. But it was definitely Caroline, and she was looking at a display of fine bone china coffee mugs.

Darcy went up beside her. "I'd suggest you not choose the ones with the gold rims."

Caroline looked up with a smile.

In the two days since Darcy had seen her last, Caroline's lip had returned almost to normal, but the dark glasses made it harder to judge the condition of her eye. If Archie's house wasn't brightly lit for the party, she just might pull it off.

"Hi, Darcy. Have you got something against gold rims?"

"They don't work very well in the microwave." Darcy's tongue was firmly in her cheek when she said it, because the very thought of Caroline, the perfect lady, microwaving a cup of water to make tea was pretty hilarious.

"They don't? Oh, of course not—the metal trim would spark. Thanks, I'd forgotten that."

Darcy was stunned. "You mean you do actually use a microwave?"

Caroline didn't answer. "Which ones do you like best?"

"If you're buying me a gift for the engagement party, then I choose the forget-me-nots."

"I should have known you'd like that design. It's utterly perfect." Caroline snagged a forget-me-not mug.

"I was joking about buying me a gift, you know. I should be getting you one for hosting this party. And what about Aunt Archie? Should I take her some kind of hostess thing?"

"There isn't a thing in the world that Aunt Archie wants—and if she does by some miracle discover something that has so far escaped her, she goes out immediately and buys it. Besides, between birthdays, holidays and hostess gifts, she could open a knickknack shop."

"Still," Darcy began.

"Trust me. Where Aunt Archie is concerned, you're the gift." Caroline had loaded her arms with a half dozen mugs, all hand-painted with floral designs. "But that reminds me, I'm awfully glad I ran into you. Archie suggested we come early tomorrow—you and I."

"To help set things up for the party? Sure. Just tell me when."

"Not exactly—she's having her masseur, her manicurist and her hairdresser come in, and she thought we might as well make a spa afternoon of it before the real event starts."

"Aunt Archie has her own masseur?"

"I'm sure he has other customers, but now that you mention it, he does seem to be available whenever she calls."

Trey came up to them, and Caroline offered her cheek. He had to bend low to get around the hat brim.

"I see it's china today," Caroline said brightly. "Are you looking at silver and crystal, too? How lovely—now I can tell everyone at the party that you're registered at Kentwells."

"Don't you think they could have guessed that much, Caroline?" Trey asked.

"I could have told them, but until there's actually something on your list to choose, what's the point? But now that you'll be selecting patterns…"

Great, Darcy thought. *That will be something else to do—return truckloads of wedding gifts.* Of course, if everyone made their purchases at Trey's store, he could take care of it with ease.

Caroline asked, "Have you set a date yet? People are starting to ask me."

"Christmas Eve," Trey said, and winked at Darcy.

Caroline frowned. "You're going to wait that long? But after this morning, I thought…"

Darcy bit her tongue. *This is where you landed us,* she wanted to tell Trey. *You and your so-funny joke about her catching us in bed together.* Well, fine—he'd gotten them into the mess by insisting that Caroline would know better than to think that going to bed together meant they were actually serious about turning the pretense into reality. Now he could get them out of it. "I'm just going to leave you two to chat, and start looking at the crystal," she said. "See you tomorrow, Caroline."

Caroline leaned forward to plant a kiss on Darcy's cheek. "I'm really glad about how this is all turning out," she said. "I like you so much, Darcy. Doesn't it seem that it was just meant to be?"

Darcy hadn't been at Aunt Archie's house for fifteen minutes before she realized that Trey not only hadn't gotten them out of the mess, but he seemed to have made things worse. Caroline was having her feet hot-waxed and chatting about wedding plans. Aunt Archie was having a facial and taking in every word. And Darcy was lying on her stomach on the massage table, doing her level best to relax enough that the masseur could do her some good.

"Madam is very tense," the masseur murmured.

How perceptive, Darcy thought. She must be as rigid as a wooden marionette, lying there.

"It's not all that long until the wedding," Aunt Archie said. "And Christmas Eve is going to be a very tough time to find a church and a reception hall."

Darcy raised her head enough to answer. "We were thinking about something much smaller."

The masseur put a hand on the back of her neck and pressed her down against the table.

"Family only?" Archie said. "Well, that makes sense— if you don't invite any business associates at all, fewer people will get their noses out of joint. How about having it here? We'll put up a couple of big Christmas trees in the drawing room and use them as a background."

"Much different from the usual arch of roses," Caroline said.

Darcy could almost smell the Scotch pines, feel the warmth of the lights, hear the laughter of the most intimate friends and family and the solemn voice of the judge. Though she'd never really thought much about a wedding—the possibility of having her own had always seemed so far off that there was no point in planning—now that the picture was brought into focus for her, she couldn't imagine anything else.

It felt so right—and so impossible—that a wave of conflicting emotions made her feel dizzy, and she gripped the edges of the table.

What's the matter with you? she thought. She understood the part about being impossible, but how could it possibly feel right to envision herself wearing a simple but elegant white satin dress trimmed in marabou, exchanging vows with Trey in front of the twinkling lights of a pair of Christmas trees?

She was out of her mind, that was all. Caught up in the feminine excitement that was connected to every wedding. And perhaps, when it came right down to it, she *had* dreamed of the wedding she wanted—even though she'd told herself not to get in a hurry. Even though she'd known quite well that she and Pete would have to wait until their business was established, until they were on a secure financial footing...

Yes, that must be why she was having such clear flashes now, like still photos popping up on a screen, because deep in her heart she'd already planned it after all.

"You should probably ask Trey what he thinks," Aunt Archie said. Her mask was beginning to set up, and her voice sounded tight. "But unless you have another place in mind already..."

Like where? Darcy thought. *The penthouse?* She almost laughed at the idea.

"What's he doing today?" Aunt Archie went on.

Darcy opened her mouth to answer before she realized that she didn't know. She'd left Trey's place this morning, checked at the cottage to find a floor half-laid and a couple of workmen scurrying around madly, and gone to the store in a last-minute desperate hunt for something to wear to the engagement party. She had no idea what his plans for the day included.

"He's playing golf with Dave," Caroline said. "He promised they'd be here in plenty of time, though—tuxedos and all."

Darcy could hardly believe her ears. "He conned *Dave* into putting on a tux?"

"I wonder if he's going to have a photographer here tonight," Caroline mused. "It would make a great picture for an ad. Have you seen the one in today's paper?"

"No. Why am I always the last to see these things?"

"Because you don't want to look at yourself," Caroline said. "I know the feeling. But the picture's really rather good." She padded carefully across the room, her feet encased in plastic booties to protect the hot wax while it cooled, and called to Gregory to bring in the newspapers.

The butler appeared only moments later, and Caroline folded the paper and held it at an angle by the massage table so Darcy could get a look. She could hardly believe her eyes.

The biggest picture on the page was of her snapping a towel at Trey. The next largest showed her putting the towels back, with Trey laughing as he held her up to the arch.

Jason had approved this? Surely not. And yet... She recalled the careless conversation she'd had with the art director. *If Jason thought the pictures would embarrass me, he'd probably run with them...*

She looked at the ad again. In the picture where Trey was holding her off the ground, her dress was bunched up and her hair was tousled. She could almost see Jason's glee when he chose it.

"Oh, man," she groaned. "This is not good."

"Yes, it is," Caroline said. "It makes you look real— and it's much better than that stodgy arrangement from yesterday. But just wait till the television ads start to play." And she smiled.

* * *

The crowd at the party seemed to agree; the towel-snapping ad was one of the main topics of conversation. When the sixth man in a row told Trey that he'd better watch out or he'd be kept in line with a towel for the next thirty years, Darcy felt her smile starting to freeze.

"Is it just me, or doesn't that line sound as funny as it did the first time?" Trey asked.

"I noticed that, too." Darcy sipped her champagne. "I wonder whether Jason will be pleased at the good response to the ad or livid because he intended to make me look like a fool."

"You'll soon find out. Here he comes."

She swung around just in time to see Jason cutting his way through Aunt Archie's living room like a battleship on a mission, straight toward her and Trey. She took a deep breath. This was probably not going to be pleasant to watch.

But it wasn't Trey that Jason confronted. Instead he pulled up directly in front of Darcy. "I told you to keep your fingers out of my advertising department," he said.

She was stunned. "I don't even know what you're talking about."

"You told the art director to go with the picture of the towels."

The magnitude of the miscommunication was more than Darcy could take in. Had the art director heard her wrong? Or had he dodged and shifted the blame when Jason confronted him?

"No, she didn't," Trey intervened. "I did."

Darcy stared at him openmouthed. "*You* approved it? Why?"

At the same instant, Jason said, "You went over my head?"

"Because it was more effective than what you'd planned," Trey said. "If you'll excuse us, Darcy, Jason and I will take this discussion to a more private place."

"Sure," she managed to say.

For an instant, when Jason had started to sound off, the party had seemed to go suddenly quiet—or had that only been the shock she'd experienced? The band out on the terrace was taking a break, and the string quartet was playing a very soft Bach air which no one seemed to be listening to. The noise levels were rising again, and she could pick out only bits of conversations from the groups around her. A group of store employees were over by the fireplace, apparently making bets on who would win the confrontation between Trey and Jason.

Nearby, Caroline was straightening the lapel of a man who had his back turned to Darcy. "Thank you for wearing the tuxedo for me," she said, and the man put an arm around her shoulders.

Something in Caroline's voice—she sounded like a little girl who'd gotten the best birthday gift of her life—made Darcy look more closely, and then she blinked and looked again. "Dave?" she gasped.

He heard her and turned. "Hi, Darcy. How's the belle of the ball doing?"

"Feeling pretty well wrung-out. Jason and Trey—" She waved a hand toward the terrace where they'd disappeared.

"I heard," Dave said.

"Don't worry about it," Caroline chimed in. "Maybe Jason will get so teed off he'll quit."

"I don't understand. If he and Trey have such differences, why do they even try to work together?"

Caroline shrugged. "It's all because of how the store structure is set up. The original partners made sure that control would always be kept in the family. Trey's from the senior branch, but if he steps down, Jason will be the president." She looked up at Dave. "Have I got it right?"

"I really can't give an opinion, Caroline."

Darcy said slowly, "So it's to Jason's advantage to agitate the situation in the hope that Trey will give up?"

"Apparently he thinks so," Caroline said. "Dave, would you get me another glass of champagne? What did Trey think about having the wedding here, Darcy?"

"I haven't asked him." As Dave walked away, Darcy lowered her voice. Though surrounded by people, for the moment they were almost alone in a bubble, and it was the first chance she'd had all day to talk to Caroline in anything resembling privacy. "Frankly it didn't seem to matter what he thought, since there isn't going to be a wedding. Caroline, you know perfectly well that whatever Trey says, this is only a charade."

Caroline smiled. "Oh, really?"

Darcy sighed in frustration. "You're a hopeless romantic, you know. And we weren't actually... Oh, never mind." She let her gaze flick across the room, catching a half-familiar face. It took her a moment to identify the man, and then she smiled. Trey had gotten his way after all— Caroline had invited the chairman of Tyler-Royale to the party.

He smiled back and said something to the woman beside him, and they slowly made their way across the room toward Darcy.

"Ross Clayton," he said, holding out a hand.

"I remember you, of course."

"And my wife, Kelly."

The woman by his side shook Darcy's hand. "You're quite the media star these days, Ms. Malone. If the response of the general public is anything like I was hearing around the country club today, you'd better prepare yourself."

"For what?"

Kelly Clayton smiled. "They'll expect to own your life. The next thing they'll want to see is pictures of the honeymoon, and then they'll want to know which crib you and Trey will pick out, and then it'll be a preschool. Probably even a college, before it's over."

I wouldn't mind a bit, Darcy thought.

For an instant, the thought was so natural that it didn't even dawn on her what was going through her mind. And when it did, the knowledge struck with the force of a wrecking ball.

She would love to pick out a crib, with Trey. A preschool, with Trey. A college, with Trey. *Anything,* with Trey.

She wanted all those things. But most of all, she wanted Trey.

This is only a charade, she'd told Caroline just minutes ago, and Caroline had given her a knowing little smile. Now she understood what Caroline had meant. Trey's sister might be a hopeless romantic, but she had obviously realized what was going on long before Darcy did. Caroline had seen that in the midst of this business deal—this arrangement which assured that whatever happened there would be no happy-ever-after ending—Darcy had fallen in love.

And clearly there was nothing she could do now but smile and carry on, and pretend it hadn't happened.

CHAPTER NINE

THEY had made a deal, and Darcy was stuck with it. She had promised not to take the pretense seriously, promised not to get caught up in the idea that this could ever be real.

And she'd lasted just short of a week.

She'd blown it big time, no doubt about that. Now she was going to have to play a role in earnest. She was going to have to be the Darcy Malone he'd proposed to in the beginning—the one who had choked at the very idea, argued against it, been flippant at the notion of love at first sight...

Well, for what it was worth, she *still* didn't believe in love at first sight. Quite.

She was going to have to pretend to be that woman for at least the next three months. The ad campaign had only started—they were too far along to back out, but not nearly far enough that simply gritting her teeth and exerting will-power would get her through.

Once the rush of photography for the ad campaign was over, things would surely ease up. But that didn't mean it would be simple. She was facing three months of the busiest social season in the city. Twelve weeks of engagement events, family get-togethers, holiday parties, goodwill and friendly kisses under the mistletoe. Ninety days of pretending to everyone in public to be Trey Kent's adoring fiancée, while at the same time pretending to him in private that she was nothing of the sort—and that she didn't want to be.

And all the time the truth would lie somewhere in the middle. She wasn't really his fiancée, and she wasn't fool enough to be adoring—she had a pretty shrewd notion of what his faults were and exactly where they lay. But loving someone had nothing to do with believing he was perfect. It was only when the faults were known and accepted that love could truly take root.

You sound like a really bad country singer, she told herself.

"Are you all right?" Kelly Clayton asked.

"Just a bit of a headache."

"I can believe it, now that you realize what you've let yourself in for. Your house will be a tourist attraction, every time you're seen in public your clothes will be reviewed, every party you give will be critiqued—"

The woman was perceptive, no doubt about it—but at least she hadn't seen through to what was really bothering Darcy. That was one small blessing.

"Stop it, Kelly," her husband said, "before she screams and runs. Darcy isn't planning to be a model forever—and people will eventually forget."

I wonder if I'll be able to forget, Darcy thought bleakly.

"I understand you're also a very talented graphic artist," he went on.

Darcy wondered how he could possibly know that. "I'm planning to open my own firm."

"Really?"

"You seem surprised at the idea."

"Well, yes. I thought I'd seen a job application cross my desk."

Would those early, sent-by-mistake packages ever stop haunting her? Darcy held on to her composure. "Yes, I did send some out while I was still exploring the options for starting up my own firm."

"Keeping all your alternatives open," Ross Clayton said.

"It's a sensible approach, don't you think?" She changed tactics, trying to distract him. "I'm just surprised you'd have seen my application, because usually human resources or the personnel office takes care of that kind of thing rather than passing it on to the CEO.''

"They do." He sipped his champagne. "I only see the most interesting candidates.''

Interesting. Well, that left a lot of room for interpretations, and most of them had nothing to do with talent. Darcy wondered if some on-the-ball personnel manager had caught the name and passed the paperwork along to the boss, not because of her qualifications but because of her connection with Trey. She wouldn't be surprised; business was business, after all.

"I'm disappointed," he went on. "I had hoped to talk to you about possibilities at Tyler-Royale.''

Darcy's face felt stiff, but she managed to force it into a smile. "You'd hire your biggest competitor's fiancée?''
That's right; keep the tone sounding amused.

"If she was the right person for the job, yes.''

"Thank you. When I get my office up and running, I'll be in touch—perhaps we can work together then.''

"I'll look forward to it. In the meantime, I need to catch Trey for a minute. If you'll excuse us?'' He lifted his glass to Darcy, and the couple moved off.

When I get my office up and running…

She'd said it almost without thinking. But now that she stopped to think about it, she knew that too was in doubt because of the blast of realization which had just hit her.

It was going to be difficult enough to get through the next ninety days as Trey's fiancée, but to continue a relationship after that would be tougher yet. To consult him about office space and financing, to talk over business plans and accounts, to work with him on projects for the stores, as she had so blithely talked about doing, when all the while she wanted things to be on a more personal level…

No. She couldn't carry it off, and so it would be better

to cut off the whole idea of a business partnership at the first possible moment.

The trouble was, that moment wouldn't come around for ninety days yet. Three endless months. Because if she said anything now, Trey would ask what on earth had changed her mind. And then what was she going to tell him? Certainly not the truth—that she'd given up the idea because she'd been foolish enough to fall in love with him. Because she wanted him to be not a business colleague but a very different kind of partner.

So in the meantime, she was going to be playing roles on multiple levels. It was enough to make her head throb in earnest.

Caroline had come up beside her once more, but it sounded to Darcy as if she were talking at the wrong speed—slow and low and too drawling to understand. "I'm sorry," Darcy said. "What was that again?"

"It's hell, isn't it?" Caroline snagged another glass of champagne from the tray of a passing waiter and shoved it into Darcy's hand. "It's really confusing to sort it all out when you're on the rebound."

Darcy's jaw dropped. "But—" How could Caroline possibly know that anything had changed in the last few minutes, since she'd shared that knowing little smile and that soft and intimate *Oh, really?* And even if she'd noted shock in Darcy's face just now, what had made her attribute the problem to being on the rebound?

"Dave told me about your fiancé," Caroline went on.

"He did *what?*"

Obviously her surprise registered with Caroline. "Ex-fiancé, I mean. Oh, he wasn't gossiping, Darcy. Dave was very kind about it—he was only telling me in order to illustrate why it was far too soon for me to think I'm falling in love with him."

Darcy's head was spinning. "Falling in love with whom? *Pete?* He's still in San Francisco."

"Of course not, silly. I mean Dave. Only he doesn't think it's really love. He believes it's too soon after Corbin for me to be attracted to anybody."

Darcy's headache had turned into a barn-burner. "What about Ginger?"

"That's over."

"He broke up with her?"

"Maybe not officially. But if he hasn't, he will."

Caroline seemed utterly confident. But did she actually know what she was talking about? Just a week ago she'd been planning to marry a man who'd turned out to be capable of battering her. Now she thought she was in love with Dave...

She's right about one thing, Darcy thought. *It's hell to try to sort it all out.*

But maybe Caroline had hit on something. Maybe Darcy wasn't really in love with Trey at all, just confused and on the rebound because of being dumped.

That would be a comfort, she told herself. It would be far easier to cope with, if she wasn't in love at all but still recuperating from the shock of her business partner and fiancé marrying the daughter of their wealthiest client.

But the idea didn't ring true. Yes, she'd been in a fog for a while over Pete's betrayal—what woman wouldn't have been?—but she'd realized after a while that what she was feeling was more anger and hurt over losing everything she'd invested in their business than anything to do with a broken heart. And if she didn't regret the breakup, then she couldn't possibly be on the rebound. It was as simple as that.

So when she'd agreed, that day in the kitchen at the cottage, to pretend to be Trey Kent's fiancée, it hadn't had anything to do with Pete. But what she hadn't realized till just now was that she hadn't agreed because of Trey's promise to set her up in business, either. It wasn't the idea of losing the chance of her own business which she'd found upsetting just now, it was the idea of losing Trey.

Even then, on the day she'd met him, it had been Trey who fascinated her. Only Trey. No wonder she'd been so confused that day, puzzled at why she'd agreed to something she'd had no intention of taking part in...

Which left her right back where she'd started, except that she now knew what she'd do about it if Trey showed any inclination to be uncooperative along the way.

She would simply threaten to go right ahead and marry him—just like the women he hadn't wanted to be engaged to—and he would fall straight back into line.

When Darcy woke up in Trey's king-sized bed on Sunday morning, there was not a sound from anywhere in the apartment except the soft rasp of her oversized T-shirt against the crisp sheets as she moved—which in contrast to the silence which surrounded her seemed absurdly loud. Trey must have gone out.

It was late, she saw by the bedside clock—but then it had been well past the wee hours when the party had finally broken up and she'd tumbled into bed. And even then, she hadn't gone straight to sleep because she'd been too haunted by the sudden, blinding realization of what she'd done.

She'd fallen in love. And she had no one but herself to blame.

Trey had been nothing but honest from the beginning— almost painfully so, she reflected, remembering that first conversation about why he'd chosen her and not some woman who he already knew. And he had never romanced her, or wooed her into falling for him. The nice things he'd done—and there had been plenty of them—had all been undertaken purely for effect, because it would look good to observers.

But Darcy hadn't listened to her head, only to her heart, and she'd allowed herself to see only what she wanted to see. Things like how compatible they were, and how much fun he was, and how very alive she felt when she was with him.

And now she would pay the price.

Well, the first step was to make herself a cup of coffee. Then she'd sit and drink it and reflect, decide what she was going to do. How she was going to get herself through the next ninety days.

At least she had the blessing of a little time and space to do her thinking, because Trey hadn't bothered her this morning.

She almost wished that he had. And she wondered what she would have done, if he'd popped his head in this morning with coffee and a bagel.

"Probably given myself away," she muttered. She should be grateful that he'd gone out somewhere.

What had Trey said he would be doing today, anyway? Or had he told her anything at all about his plans? Perhaps he hadn't—but then there was no particular reason he should. If she'd still been living in the penthouse, he certainly wouldn't call her up to say he was going out for a bike ride or to buy a Sunday paper. She wouldn't have any idea whether he was at home, at the store, or on the golf course.

It was just one more illustration—as if she needed another reminder—that the situation she was living in wasn't real.

At least, she should be able to go back to the penthouse today. If Dave's office was to be open as usual tomorrow, then surely Mrs. Cusack's desk would be moved away from the doorway by tonight, and she could get upstairs to her clothes.

Clothes—that was one more thing she should do today, she thought. If she used the washer and dryer in Trey's kitchen, she wouldn't have to bother going to the laundry next week. She gathered up the few things she'd brought with her, and the extras she'd bought in order to carry her through the weekend, and headed for the kitchen. She'd start a load now—just in case he turned up and had plans for the day—and then she'd go get dressed.

Just in case he had made plans which included her.

It wasn't simply wishful thinking, Darcy told herself. Not exactly. Trey might have some public show in mind to follow up the spectacle of the engagement party last night. But it would certainly be foolish to let herself believe that she herself was the attraction, if he wanted her by his side.

She stopped dead at the edge of the living room. Trey was sitting on the leather couch, reading the newspaper and drinking coffee. "Good morning," he said cheerfully. "I ordered brunch. It should be coming along any minute now."

Darcy clutched her laundry to her chest. "I...I should get dressed."

"Why? After last night, you deserve an easy day. If you want to sit around in pajamas, I won't object."

"I'm not wearing pajamas."

He smiled. "I noticed that. It's a very nice T-shirt—it always was one of my favorites, but I sure never looked that tasty in it."

She doubted that. He looked pretty good to her in jeans, in sweat pants, in a suit, in... *Stop it,* she warned herself, *before you get to contemplating him wearing nothing at all.*

"There will be a lot of cleaning up to do," Darcy said. "Aunt Archie was kind enough to let us use the house, so we shouldn't leave her with a mess."

"You don't really think Caroline would have forgotten about the cleanup."

"But I should help her."

"I didn't say she'd be doing it herself. I'll guarantee the caterer took care of the last stirring stick and blotted napkin about the time the sun rose, while Caroline—and Archie, for that matter—were peacefully tucked into their beds."

"Oh." Darcy put the bundle of laundry down in a chair and sat on the opposite end of the couch from him, pulling her feet up under her. "I guess I'm showing that I belong in the other half of society. I never gave a party where I didn't have to clean up afterward."

Trey's forehead wrinkled. "What's the matter, Darcy? Did someone say something rude to you last night to make you believe you didn't fit in that crowd?"

"No."

"Then what happened?" He let the silence draw out. "I saw you talking to Ross and Kelly Clayton."

"Only about the possibility that he might have me do some work for him." Too late, Darcy remembered the decision she'd made last night about her business. It probably wasn't smart even to bring the subject up right now, to open herself to questions. On the other hand, what else could she tell him about her conversation with the Claytons? That they'd been discussing cribs and preschools?

Not that she expected that the topic would upset him; he'd probably find it extraordinarily funny. And having him laugh at the idea would be absolutely the last straw for Darcy.

"Hey," he said lightly, "I thought you were waiting for me to be your first client. We need to talk about that, by the way. Have you thought about a location?"

Yes. But that had been before last night. "Not really. It's just been too busy, Trey."

"Well, you need to get started. It takes more than a name

and a logo before you can start up a business. There will be months of planning.''

Darcy bit her lip. This was turning out to be a simply delightful conversation. If she dodged the subject, she would look like the dilettante he'd originally thought she was—a starry-eyed dreamer who thought that owning her own firm meant not having to really work at all. But if she answered his questions and shared the plans she'd already made, she'd be committing herself to a future she no longer wanted. The more she told him about her ideas and the work she'd already done to prepare herself, the more difficult it would be to convince him eventually that she'd changed her mind...

Caught like a bug in a spiderweb. Whatever I do, I'll just make everything stickier.

''I've been looking into it,'' Trey said. ''What I've found out so far—''

To Darcy's relief, the doorbell rang and Trey went to answer it. He came back pushing a miniature steam table on wheels and maneuvered it into place by the corner of the dining room table. ''Let's eat,'' he said. ''All those dainty nibbles Caroline served last night left me starving for some real food.''

''I see that,'' Darcy said, surveying the contents of the cart. Waffles, scrambled eggs, potatoes, sausage and bacon, biscuits and gravy... ''Am I seeing things, or is that really a platter of barbecued ribs?''

''Best ones in the city.'' He held her chair and handed her a plate. ''Dig in—I ordered plenty. What were we talking about?''

''Breakfast,'' she said firmly, hoping to deflect him.

''Oh, no. We were discussing your business. You said you wanted to get started, so I've been asking around, investigating the field. You'd have an awfully lot of competition. I had no idea there were so many graphic artists in Chicago.''

"Competition goes with the territory," she said. She reached for a slice of toast. "Besides, they're not all good ones, and they have different specialties."

"If you seriously think you're going to be able to pick and choose your jobs—"

"Come on, Trey. I'm not completely unrealistic. Of course I'll have to—" She bit back the protest. Maybe it was better to leave it like this. What difference did it make if he thought she was some visionary who was too out of touch with the business world to recognize the basic truth that owning a business didn't make someone independent? Why should it matter if he thought she was a fool?

Because I want him to think well of me, she admitted.

Things would have been so much easier, Darcy thought wistfully, if she had never met Trey at all. If only he had never brought Caroline to consult with Dave... If only Mrs. Cusack hadn't had sinus trouble that day...

She munched her toast, thinking dreamily of the way things would have been if Trey hadn't come into her life. She'd be waking up in the penthouse this morning—because without that original consultation, there would never have been a spilled glass of wine and therefore no need to replace the carpet. By now, Darcy would have sent out another couple of batches of job applications, and with any luck at all, she'd have some interviews coming up this week...

She might even have gotten a call from someone at the Kentwells chain, and met Trey after all.

No matter where she tried to send her thoughts, she always ended up with Trey on her mind.

You're fooling yourself, Darcy.

Not meeting Trey might have made her life slightly less

complicated, but it certainly wouldn't have been as interesting. This was going to hurt when it was over—for that matter, it was hurting quite enough already. But she wouldn't trade the gift of knowing him, even if by doing so she could make the rest of her life pain-free.

She knew that particular philosophy didn't make sense. If she had never met him, then she would never have had any idea what she'd missed. Still, just the thought of not ever having known him felt as if someone had drilled a hole through her heart.

"Darcy," he said. "You're scaring me, honey—looking like that."

She caught herself up short. Letting her thoughts drift was dangerous. Fortunately he was sitting at an angle next to her and not straight across the table. Still, what might he have seen in her eyes, in her face, in her expression, in her body language? Longing? Pain? *Love?*

And what would he have to say about it?

"Looking like what?" she asked warily.

He picked up a rib and turned it over, apparently looking for the meatiest first bite. "Like you're finished with the toast, and now you're about to start going after live prey."

She choked on the last bite. "You wish."

He looked at her over the rib and smiled, that stunning, sexy, devastating smile that brightened the room, lit up his eyes and made her feel far more steamy and breathless than the bright photographic lights did. "Well, yeah," he said. "I do wish that. What are the chances?"

"Of me attacking you? What would you do?"

Trey looked thoughtful. "I guess the first thing I'd do would be to put the top back on the steam table to keep the food warm, and then I'd let you chase me."

She sat very still while he ate his rib.

It would be foolish to get any more involved. In fact, it

would be criminally stupid to seduce him. She would only be adding to the eventual pain.

But she would also be adding to the stock of pleasant memories that would help her bear the pain. And for once—even if only for a little while—she would be the total focus of his attention.

She pushed her chair back. It skidded on the carpet and she almost lost her balance. She had to take hold of the edge of the table to steady herself, and the walk around the steam table to his side seemed to take forever.

He put the rib down on his plate. "Are you serious?"

"Deadly," she said. "Don't bother to wipe off your fingers."

He curved an arm around her waist, pulled her down onto his lap and kissed her long and deeply. She had practically melted by the time he was finished, and any doubts she'd had about the essential rightness of what she was doing had faded into oblivion. Tomorrow, next week, or in ninety days—when it would all be over—she might regret this. But not now.

He held her an inch away from him. "Maybe I should ask…" He sounded breathless.

She looked straight at him. "Yes, Trey, I really want to do this. I really want to make love with you."

"Good. I'm glad to hear it. But that wasn't what I wanted to know."

She felt just a bit dizzy and she was having trouble sitting up straight. "Fine time to get curious. What is it?"

"I just need to know if you're being a praying mantis, or a black widow spider."

She smiled. "Neither. You said yourself I'm a rattlesnake."

"Well, that's a relief—since rattlesnakes don't consume their mates after making love."

"Though I suppose there's a first time for everything," she murmured.

"Then I guess I'll just have to make sure you're otherwise satisfied." He slid an arm under her knees and lifted her off his lap. As he stood up, his chair went over backward, but neither of them paid any attention. And he didn't put the cover back on the steam table.

He carried her into the bedroom, and Darcy stretched out luxuriously on the bed and reached up for him as he shed his jeans and disposed of her T-shirt. "I have to tell you, Trey, that wasn't much of a chase you led me on there."

"Yeah, well, I wouldn't want you to be too exhausted to catch me." He slid under the sheet next to her. "Or, for that matter, in need of nourishment afterward."

And then the silliness gave way to tenderness and nurturing, to exploring and enjoying, and finally to soaring and crashing on the tide of passion.

Darcy must have slept a little, for when she stirred and realized where she was, she was as limp as a rag doll, half-draped across his body. Trey was fully relaxed, too, his fingertips lazily toying with her hair.

"I'm starving," Darcy said huskily.

Trey raised his head warily. "The urge for self-preservation requires me to ask what you're hungry for, before I agree to anything."

"Ribs."

"That's fine, then. I told you they're the best ones in the city."

"I don't doubt it."

"And you already have a smear of barbecue sauce on your face, so you may as well—"

She wasn't listening. She stretched out a hand to splay across his chest. "Best ribs in the city. I heard it from a reliable source." She ran her fingertips up and down as if his rib cage formed the strings of a harp and then bent her head to nibble at the taut flesh. "And I don't need any sauce."

"Right," Trey said. "But I have an even better idea. Let me show you."

Darcy didn't go back to the penthouse—but on Monday morning, feeling deliciously relaxed and in tune with the world, she refused a ride to work with Trey. "Go ahead to your meeting," she said. "I'm going to have another cup of coffee, and when I get there I'll look around the store for a gift for Aunt Archie—just a little thank-you for hosting the party."

Trey was standing in the kitchen, finishing his second cup. His tie was still loose around his neck, but in every other way he was as polished and well-tailored as ever. Darcy tried not to smile at the contrast between this man and the lover of just a couple of hours ago, when he'd still been stubbly and tousled—and incredibly sexy.

"If you're giving anyone a thank-you gift," Trey said, "make it Gregory. He did a lot more of the work than Aunt Archie did, that's for sure." He set his cup down and gave her a long, lingering kiss.

After he was gone, she sat for a long time thinking. Reason told her it would be wise not to take anything for granted. There was no question in her mind that Trey didn't mean anything long-term to come of this—heaven knew he'd declared as much on several occasions, and he hadn't said anything yesterday or last night, even in the heat of passion, which contradicted that idea.

No, she wasn't idiot enough to think that sleeping with her meant he had anything permanent in mind. But what she was considering right now was the short-term. Very short-term. Like—today.

A sensible woman would pack up her things and move back to the penthouse. The invitation to stay with him had been issued for as long as it took to get the flooring in the cottage done and the furniture back in place, and that job must be finished by now. It would be better if she didn't assume that anything had changed.

And yet, if she went back home, surely she would give up any chance of this...whatever it was...turning into something more. Something deeper. Something more like love.

Exactly, she told herself rudely. Which was why the sooner she did it, the better—since there was precisely no chance of it coming to anything, no matter what she did. Far better to leave on her own than to have him suggest that it was time for her to go home.

So—feeling rather sad about it, but knowing it was the only logical thing to do—she gathered her things and put them in her car.

She was startled to find that the mall parking lot was almost full. Surely that was unusual for a Monday morning. But she was even more surprised to see that most of the traffic was not at the Tyler-Royale end of the shopping complex but outside Kentwells. She had to park more than halfway down the lot, not far from Tyler-Royale, so she went in the mall entrance rather than directly to the store.

At least she could tell Trey that she hadn't actually walked through the competition's aisles, she thought with a smile, and caught herself up short when someone called her name.

Ross Clayton was just coming out of the Tyler-Royale store. "Good to see you this morning," he said. "But I don't suppose you're coming this direction."

"Sorry. I'd only be comparison-shopping anyway."

"Go ahead. I don't think we'd come off badly. Mind if I walk along with you for a ways?"

"Not at all. I'm surprised to see you here—I thought Trey said your office was downtown."

"It is. But this store is between managers at the moment, so until the new one can get his affairs wound up in Seattle and get moved, I'm helping to fill the gap. He's here as much as he can be, but he's trying to help the new person in Seattle get settled, and—"

"It sounds complex."

"Something like working a jigsaw puzzle inside a black bag, where you can't see the pieces at all."

"Trey's got things easier with just having stores here in the city."

"It's easier in one sense, with his focus all in one geographical location. Harder in other ways, because if the local economy takes a downturn, he doesn't have another city's sales to balance it out."

"Yes, I see." Impulsively she asked, "Did you mean it when you said you'd hire me?"

"Sure."

She took a deep breath. It felt important to do something now—right away—to assure her future. And, she thought, to remind herself that no matter how real this engagement might feel, it wasn't going to last. "Would you be willing to wait for me to take the job till Christmas?"

His gaze was shrewd. "Till this ad campaign is over?"

"Yes." Darcy bit her lip, and then said, "I need to tell you something—in confidence."

He nodded.

"If you're thinking of hiring me because I'm going to be married to the CEO of the Kentwells chain, then don't."

"I'd be hiring you for who you are, Darcy."

"I need to be very clear about this. You should know before you make the decision that I won't have any connection with the stores after Christmas, because—the engagement will be over then, too."

There was a long pause, and then Ross smiled. "So it's true. Trey made the whole thing up."

"No, he didn't. Not really. I mean, it was going to be Caroline, but then all of a sudden…'' Darcy stumbled, remembering that what had happened to Caroline wasn't her story to tell.

But Ross wasn't listening anyway. They'd reached the food court, and he raised a hand in greeting to a man who was sitting at a table near the coffee bar.

Trey.

"Let's talk about it later, Darcy,'' Ross said. "But you can be assured of a job whenever you want one.''

Trey had stood up. "What's this about? Are you guys getting to be pals?''

"Just cutting a little deal on the side, Trey,'' Ross said. "I have to congratulate you, you know. It was a pretty cunning move to start that ad campaign right now, improving the public image of your stores just in time to increase the price I'm willing to pay for them. Well, let's see what sort of an agreement we can make.''

Trey shot a look at Darcy, who felt sick. She had, unwittingly, given him away. She had forgotten the cardinal rule of business—never forget who you're talking to—and shared sensitive information with Trey's biggest competitor. The man who was trying to buy him out at the best possible price now knew that he could offer less and get more for his money…

But why hadn't Trey told her what was going on? Why hadn't he trusted her? She'd never have breathed a word if she'd only realized how important it was that Ross Clayton not know the truth.

Don't try to excuse yourself, Darcy. Nobody was supposed to know.

Then she took a closer look at Trey. His face was set, but not in anger at her. He looked guilty.

It was a cunning move to start that ad campaign right now…

And suddenly she saw the truth which had lain hidden all along, behind the engagement and the ad campaign. He hadn't been trying to protect Caroline from publicity or embarrassment by stepping in to take her place. He hadn't even been trying to keep a planned ad campaign running smoothly for the sake of the stores.

The entire thing had been planned from the beginning. It had been nothing more than a ploy to bring up the sale price of the Kentwells chain. And Darcy had been only a tool—near at hand when Caroline had no longer been useful.

She had unintentionally given Trey away, and she was sorry for making his job harder. But what she had done had been a mistake, an innocent miscalculation.

His action had been deliberate. He had used her—and that was something she could not forgive.

CHAPTER TEN

TREY had used her, just as her ex-fiancé had used her. The only difference between Trey and Pete was that this time she'd found out before he was finished. Before he'd had the chance to dump her.

She smiled, doing her best to make it seem real. "I'll leave you two to your discussion," she said. "See you later, Trey."

Sheer pride allowed her to keep her spine straight as she walked away—not back toward the entrance as she wanted to, for that would tell him for certain that she'd seen through his game, and he might come after her. Instead she strolled away down the mall toward the Kentwells store—the same way she would have done if she'd been carrying out her original plan, to buy Aunt Archie a hostess gift and then get ready for today's round of photos.

There was no doubt she would have to talk to him sometime. But if she could just have an hour or two to get her head together, to think…

It would be at least that long before he realized she was gone. If she actually walked through the store, she might put the moment off even longer, because then when he came in, employees would say that she must be there somewhere because they'd seen her. Embarrassing herself by bursting into tears in front of the staff wasn't going to be any problem, because she was far too angry to cry. If she could just continue to hold her head up…

She tried not to break step, but as she passed the jewelry department she had no choice but to stop, for the little manager called after her. "Ms. Malone! Ms. Malone! If I could trouble you for just a moment—"

Reluctantly she turned toward the department. He was reaching into a safe built under one of the counters, scrambling to get something, and so she went on in.

"I'd like you to look at your wedding ring," he said.

So his enthusiasm had overwhelmed Trey's stalling tactics after all—unless he just meant he had another sketch prepared. But no, it was a ring that he pulled out of the locked compartment.

Her wedding ring—though in fact this was like no other ring she'd ever seen. The two bands were faithful to the design as he'd initially sketched them, but otherwise she wouldn't have recognized the ring at all. It looked very little like she'd imagined it. The gold wasn't shiny—it looked clouded. There were no jewels, only a few faint indentations where they might eventually go. The only thing which resembled a prong extended from the shank of the ring, where it would scratch the wearer's palm raw.

"It doesn't look anything like what I expected from your sketch," she said.

He smiled as if she were a particularly dull pupil. "It will when it's finished. But fresh casts are very different. This one still has the sprue." He pointed to the odd-looking prong. "That's the extra bit of gold from when it was poured into the mold. And we don't polish the metal till later in the process, either. If I might hold your ring for a moment, though—I'd like to try the two of them together and see how they look before I start polishing and setting the stones."

Darcy looked down at the amethyst on her left hand, and then she reluctantly took it off. How perfectly stupid it was to feel the pangs of regret, she told herself, for she'd always known that this moment was hanging over her head. From the instant Trey had slipped the ring on to her finger, it had been quite clear that it wouldn't stay there forever. Furthermore, she hadn't wanted it to.

Or if she had already been dreaming in that direction—as it now seemed that she had—she simply hadn't realized it yet. If it had crossed her mind, she would have written it off as an outlandish idea.

She watched as the jeweler fitted the rings together. The combination of the amethyst in its antique setting and the painfully new jacket was a study in glaring contrasts which made Darcy's eyes hurt.

The jeweler, however, seemed to have no problem visualizing the finished product, and judging by the little crowing noises he was making, he was thrilled with how his work was turning out. "Just let me take a few measurements," he said. "I won't delay you but a moment. I want to be sure the jacket fits exactly."

"No hurry," she said, and then realized that this was her perfect opportunity. She was eager to get rid of the ring—or at least she should be, now that she knew about Trey's real agenda. "Why don't you just keep it for a while? You'll need it in order to match everything up and make it fit. And I'll just be careful my left hand doesn't show up in any pictures today."

The promise was quite sincere; the fact that she intended to keep her word by ducking out of the store rather than sticking around for any photographs at all was entirely beside the point.

He protested, but Darcy folded his hand closed over the ring set, made a feeble joke about holding him responsible for the heirloom and headed for the door as quickly as she could.

Justine wasn't at the cosmetics counter. That was one small blessing, not having to give her any excuse for walking out of the store. Darcy reached her car and sat in silence for a few minutes, wondering where she wanted to go.

She'd been too occupied for the last few minutes to think

about Trey, but now that the immediate need to perform was over, she felt herself starting to shake with anger.

How dare he not tell her the truth? How dare he not tell her that the entire performance was a charade on even more levels than he'd admitted? That he hadn't stepped into Caroline's spot in the royal wedding hoopla as a means of sheltering his sister, but purely to turn a profit?

And yet, why should he have told her everything?

You're not important, whispered a little voice in the back of her head. *You're just a hired hand. An employee. The boss doesn't tell the workers everything that's going on. He doesn't have to.*

In fact, she realized, even being angry at him was a part of loving him. If she didn't care about him, then it wouldn't have mattered so much that he'd kept a section of the story to himself, that he hadn't shared the details. It was his business, after all—not hers.

But he was important to her—and Darcy wanted to be just as important to him.

Suddenly she felt so exhausted that she could barely stand it. She started the engine and carefully drove back to the cottage.

There was a bright-red sports car parked just around the corner, not quite out of sight of the front door. She stared at it in amazement. How could Trey possibly have gotten there before her? How did he even know she was gone, or where to find her?

She thought about going on past the cottage and just driving. But there was nowhere else that she felt like going, and she figured she might as well get the confrontation over with. Maybe it would be better to do it right now, before either of them had had a chance to think or to plan what they wanted to say. While she was still too tired to care how it all turned out.

*   *   *

Trey was having trouble focusing on the numbers Ross Clayton was talking about, because he kept seeing Darcy's face rather than the paperwork lying in front of him.

He could still see the consternation in her eyes as she'd realized that she'd confided in the one person who could do the most harm with the knowledge she'd handed him, but it was the look which had come after that one which haunted him even more. Shock, dismay, hurt and loathing had been mixed together in her lovely face.

And he also couldn't forget the quick patter of her steps as she'd hurried away. The rhythm seemed to have etched itself in his brain.

"Look," Ross said. "Let's agree in principle, shake hands on the deal and leave the exact numbers till later when you can concentrate."

"I can concentrate just fine," Trey mumbled. Then he pushed his chair back. "I'm sorry, I just need a minute to…"

"I know," Ross said. "It's times like these that I wish I was a shark. If I told you that contract you're looking at was a love letter to that young woman, you'd sign it in a minute. Go get your personal life straightened out and I'll talk to you tomorrow."

Now that was a hilarious thought, Trey told himself. Not the idea that he might mistake a sales contract for a love letter, but that he'd even consider putting his name to anything of the sort… A love letter to Darcy—he'd have snorted at the very notion, if it wouldn't have been rude to the man who'd just offered him a multimillion dollar deal.

A love letter… He'd have to tell Darcy that one. She'd enjoy the story, if he could get her to stop looking at him with that mixture of hurt and loathing…

But first he had to find her, and nobody in the store seemed to know where she was. Justine hadn't seen her;

Arabella only sniffed, and the manager of the jewelry department was too much in awe of his own creation even to hear Trey ask if he'd seen Darcy.

"Look at this," the jeweler said. "How splendidly the two pieces fit together, and how the diamonds will accent the amethyst."

Trey stopped in midstep. "That's Darcy's ring."

"Yes, sir. When I showed her the jacket this morning, she offered to let me keep the amethyst so I could work on it."

"She offered to let you keep it?" Trey asked slowly. But she'd been wearing it in the food court. He'd noticed because her hand had been trembling as she reached up to push her hair back behind her ear, and the amethyst had caught the overhead lights...

So she'd come here, and she'd left her ring.

But what else had she left? The store? Him?

A love letter. No wonder the humor he'd felt over that remark had been forced and awkward. It wasn't because the idea was so ridiculous, but because it was so real.

"Dammit," he said. "Give me that ring."

The first thing Darcy noticed as she opened the front door was that the new floor was gorgeous, rich and dark and polished till it reflected almost like a mirror. The second thing she saw was a new—or rather, an antique—tea cart which held a shiny stainless steel pot and a selection of hand-painted bone china mugs in floral designs—the mugs Caroline had been buying at the Kentwells store on Friday.

The woman behind Mrs. Cusack's desk had her head bent over a file drawer behind the desk, and Darcy took a second look and croaked, "Caroline?"

"Yes, may I help—" The woman straightened up. "Oh, hi, Darcy."

"You're..." Darcy was almost speechless. "What are you doing here?"

"I'm just helping out because Mrs. Cusack's sinuses kicked up again."

"You're helping out?"

"Yes. She says it must have been all the dust that came off the carpet when the workers pulled it up, but since she hasn't been here since they took the carpet up, I have my doubts that was really the cause."

"So you're making yourself indispensable."

Caroline grinned. "Well, I do hope so. Want some coffee? It's the real stuff, not that sludge Dave makes. I forbade him to touch the new pot."

"That was an excellent move." Darcy tipped her head toward the closed door of Dave's office. "Is Trey in there?"

"Trey? No. Is he supposed to be?"

"The car's outside. But wait—it's your car, isn't it? I thought... Sorry, all that made no sense at all. Just ignore me."

Of course he couldn't have gotten across town before her. He wouldn't have tried—even if he already knew she wasn't in the store, and it was doubtful that he did. Once again, Darcy's hope had outrun her common sense. If he'd cared enough to come chasing after her so fast, then maybe she mattered after all. But it had been, of course, nothing more than a foolish hope.

"Darcy? Are you all right?"

"Never better," Darcy said. "I'm just going to get my things from the car. Would you ask Dave if he'll see me as soon as he's free?"

"Sure. I was going to check with you, by the way—I think this letterhead Dave's got is pretty tired-looking. I was thinking if you had time, maybe you'd give some thought to a new logo, new business cards, everything.

Now that we have a new look in the office, maybe it's time for a new image all the way around.''

Darcy looked at her thoughtfully. Caroline was obviously in siege mode, and Darcy wouldn't care to bet against her. Dave might think that Caroline was still on the rebound, but the woman had apparently made up her mind, and she was going to get him.

Which left Darcy with mixed feelings. She liked Caroline; in fact, she couldn't think of anyone she'd rather have as a sister-in-law. But that meant that sometimes, unavoidably, their two families would meet up. And that would put Darcy and Trey face-to-face.

She'd come home so she wouldn't ever run into Pete in San Francisco. Now she faced the almost certainty of encountering Trey in Chicago…

Maybe I'll send my next batch of job applications to the East Coast.

She was lifting her shopping bag out of her car when a small black car screeched to a halt next to her and Trey leaned out of the window. "What the hell are you doing?"

If the volume of his voice was the measuring stick of his concern, then he was off the charts where she was concerned, but Darcy suspected in this case the two things had no relationship. "Getting my stuff," she said coolly.

"Why aren't you at the store?"

She looked past him to the almost-blocked street. "Why don't you park that thing, come on in, have a cup of coffee and discuss it like reasonable people?"

"If only," he said under his breath, but he moved the car to the nearest parking spot.

"Or maybe you shouldn't come in," Darcy said as he slammed the car door hard enough that the sound echoed. "It's Caroline's first day on the job, and I'd hate for her to have to call the riot police to have you ejected."

"On the job?" He looked puzzled. "Since when is Caroline working here?"

"I thought that might get your attention." She set the bag on the hood of her car and leaned against the fender. "I assume you got your deal made?"

She couldn't stop herself from holding her breath. If he said no, that they hadn't made an agreement...if he told her that he'd put Ross Clayton on hold so he could come after her...

"Yes," Trey said. "The Kentwells chain will merge with the Tyler-Royale stores."

She felt the words like a fist clenching her lungs, and it took a minute before she could breathe quite right again. "Jason's going to hate that idea."

"He shouldn't. He'll be much better off financially than if he was managing the store, or even running the chain."

"Somehow I doubt he'll see it that way, since being in control seemed more important to him than results ever did."

"Yes. But that's why the stores have gotten into such a state, so..."

"Did I ask you to explain it to me? I really don't care, Trey." It wasn't true, of course—but right now she couldn't bear to have him talk to her like an ordinary colleague, someone who was mildly interested in the outcome but who had no great personal stake in how things turned out.

"All right," he said quietly. "I won't bother."

She let the silence drag out. *Just leave him standing here and walk on to the cottage,* she told herself. But she couldn't force herself to move. In any case, she'd rather not have a witness to this conversation, so she might as well finish it right here as have him follow her inside. "I suppose you came to ask me to go back to the store with you."

"Any reason I shouldn't? We still have a campaign to shoot."

"Do we really? I felt sure now that you'd struck a deal to sell the stores, the whole idea behind the campaign was satisfied. What was it Ross said? Something about improving the public image of the stores just in time to increase the price he was willing to pay for them. But if the price is set, then there's no need to carry on the pretense."

"Darcy—"

"Or does Ross think it's still a good idea, and now that you're working for him, you want to please the boss?" Almost in midsentence, Darcy caught herself up short. It was past time to watch what she said, or he'd be wondering why she was taking the whole thing so personally.

"What difference does it make? You agreed to shoot the campaign—and the deal I struck this morning doesn't do anything to change that. It's still a good idea."

She shrugged. "I guess I'm just sensitive that way."

"Why are you here, anyway? I looked for you at the store."

"I didn't know how long you'd be tied up."

"I thought maybe you'd gone home."

Home. What a beautiful word it was—or would have been, if only he'd meant it as she wanted him to. "I did come home, Trey," she said levelly. "This is home right now."

"You know what I mean. I went to the apartment, looking for you. All your things were gone."

"All my things?" She waved a hand at the bag. "You mean this wealth of belongings? You sound surprised that I don't want to live indefinitely out of a single shopping bag."

"I didn't ask you to leave."

"No, you didn't—and I suppose you'd have liked having

me stick around a few more days. I must admit myself that yesterday was fun.''

''There was nothing this morning to even hint that you were going.''

She shrugged. ''Well, yeah, I suppose you're right about that.''

''A roll in the hay and a kiss goodbye and then poof, you're gone.''

She couldn't stand for him to make light of what had happened between them. ''Stop it!''

''If you can dismiss it as unimportant, Darcy, then I can, too.''

She bit her lip. ''Anyway, it doesn't much matter, because then I got to the mall and found out what you've been up to all this time.''

''Yes,'' he said softly. ''And that's what I find so interesting, Darcy. There wasn't time for you to go to the apartment and pack after you left the mall, so you must have done it beforehand.''

She blinked in surprise. ''How would you know that?''

''I asked the doorman when you'd left and whether you'd come back. You must have packed up even before you saw Ross this morning. Before you knew about the deal. Why, Darcy?''

She shrugged. What did it matter, anyway? Maybe it was better if he thought she'd left because she was bored. Then he probably wouldn't bother looking beyond his wounded ego. ''Well, I did tell you I was just as skittish as you are. And it seemed a good time—even fun weekends come to an end.''

''I see.'' His voice sounded heavy. ''So none of that mattered to you.''

She should nod and agree, and let it go at that. But something deep inside wouldn't let her diminish the magic they had shared, not even to preserve her pride. ''Yes,'' she said.

"It mattered. But then when I found out what you were up to, it was obvious that I'd made the right choice anyway. I don't like being treated like a tool, Trey. You see, it isn't the first time it's happened to me—being used to make someone's business successful, without being told what my role really was."

He said quietly, "So that's why you came back here, instead of staying in San Francisco. What was his name? Pete something?"

"Pete Willis," she said unwillingly. "And I'd rather not talk about it."

He didn't move or speak. The silence grew endlessly.

Finally Darcy capitulated. "All right—if you want the dirt, I'll give it to you. I went to San Francisco with Pete to start an ad agency. He handled the sales, I did all the layouts, we worked together on the ideas."

"A partnership."

"Yes—but it was more than that. After a while, we decided that when we got the business off the ground we were going to be married. I even had the diamond to show for it. At least it looked like a diamond, and what kind of woman checks up on the engagement ring her fiancé gives her? In the meantime, we were both working our tails off to make the agency successful. I even started endorsing some of my paychecks back to the firm, to help the business grow faster."

"His idea, no doubt?"

"I don't remember. Probably." She swallowed hard, trying to get rid of the lump in her throat. "And then one day he came in from a meeting and told me that he'd made a deal with a new client—who was going to be a very big and exclusive account because Pete was going to marry the client's daughter. He offered me two weeks severance pay because his fiancée didn't want me hanging around any more, and he graciously offered to let me keep the engagement ring.''

''And that was when you found out it wasn't really a diamond.''

Darcy sighed. ''Not for a while, till I was completely out of funds. It turned out to be the finest grade imitation, so I pawned it for a hundred dollars and bought gas for the drive home. But what does all that matter? Maybe I should be getting used to being a tool. But that doesn't mean I have to like it, or make it easier.''

''I'm not your ex-fiancé, Darcy.''

Her voice was sharp. ''Oh, yes you are. *Very* ex.''

''I meant that I'm not Pete Willis.''

''No. You had a better excuse than he did.''

''Darcy—''

''He deliberately set me up—and I suppose I'm fortunate that he showed his true colors when he did, or I might have actually drifted into marrying him eventually, without ever wondering if that was really what I wanted. But you didn't even know me, so it wasn't as if you set out to smash me flat the same way that Pete did. You had no reason to tell me all your secrets. And also,'' she added thoughtfully, ''I got more out of the deal this time around.''

''An amethyst instead of a fake diamond, you mean.''

She held up her bare hand, fingers spread. ''No—the ring is at the store. I'm sorry about the wedding ring, because I suppose the manager's going to want to bill it to you. But maybe you can sell it as a set now... Anyway, I just meant I got some pretty clothes this time, and some good meals. A pleasant party, a few nice interludes in your bed...''

''Stop it, Darcy.''

''And after all, why should I have expected you to tell me all your plans? You didn't even want to tell me your name at first—*Mr. Smith*—so why should I have been surprised that you would hold a few cards close to your chest all the way through the game?''

She was asking herself, more than him, even though she knew the answer. *Because I wanted him to trust me. Because I wanted him to share.*

He didn't say anything at all.

After a bit, Darcy said, ''I think we're finished here, so if you'll just run along—''

''No, we're not finished. Not by a long shot.'' He sounded almost grim.

Her heart skipped a beat and then started fluttering like a hummingbird's wings.

''I thought there was time,'' he said, almost to himself. ''I thought there was no hurry.''

What was he saying? *Not what you want him to, she told herself. Hang on to your common sense.* ''Time?''

''Three whole months.''

''Oh. The campaign. Look, I'm sorry if your new boss wants to keep up the charade, but—'' She groped for some excuse, some reason he'd accept.

''He's *your* new boss, Darcy.''

''What?'' For a moment, she'd forgotten the agreement she'd made with Ross Clayton, because so many things had been circling in her mind ever since those moments as they'd walked up to the food court. The reminder hit like a rock straight to her chest.

She had told Ross Clayton she would work for him and the Tyler-Royale stores. She had asked him to wait for her to take the job until after Christmas, and that had prompted him to ask about the campaign. If she wasn't working on the campaign, then he would assume she was free to take a new position right away. But what if the job he had in mind was one where she had to work with Trey?

Or worse yet, Ross might even make it part of her duties to finish out the old job first, before starting a new one.

The success of Trey's campaign had already showed up in the parking lot outside the store, and no doubt in the cash registers inside as well. Why would Ross agree to interrupt that, especially when telling the truth would destroy all the interest and goodwill they'd succeeded in building up with just a few days' worth of ads?

"You made a deal," Trey reminded. "Three months."

Darcy's head hurt. "I guess you've got me there. I suppose if I have to—"

"No," Trey said softly. "You don't have to. I get the message, loud and clear. It isn't the campaign you're objecting to—nothing's changed there. It's me."

She could hardly deny that, even if she wanted to soothe his feelings. "What about Ross?" she said. "I don't imagine he'll want to hire me after this, and I understand—but what about you? Is he going to hold this against you?"

"Why did you even ask him about a job, anyway?" Trey sounded curious. "I thought you wanted your own business, your independence."

No, she thought. *I wanted you. And if I can't have you for myself, then I don't want to be your dependent.*

She shrugged. "Oh, you know. All those things you said about all the competition I'd be facing, how I couldn't choose my clients after all, how difficult it was going to be…"

"I don't believe you. That's because of me, too, isn't it?"

"Not everything is about you, Trey." At least, she wasn't about to explain that one to him. "Is it going to affect your job with Ross—if we don't go ahead with the campaign, I mean? Because I suppose I could—"

"You'd reconsider if I needed you to?"

Darcy shrugged. She wasn't sure what she'd be willing to do, when it came right down to it. She only knew that suddenly, with the end looming, she didn't want to say goodbye.

"Don't worry about it. I'm not going to work for him. My position ends when the chains merge."

"But why?"

"Because that's the condition I put on it. The original ownership of the stores was set up to keep management in the family, no matter what. As long as the family owns the stores, it must be a member of the family who runs them."

"I know. Caroline told me."

"Unfortunately the founders didn't contemplate the possibility of a generation that was uninterested—as with Caroline and me—or unqualified."

"You mean Jason?"

"Right. He stepped in on a temporary basis when my father first became ill, and it wasn't apparent for a while what was happening. Then when things started going downhill it went all at once, and the rest of the family owners—Aunt Archie among them—insisted on me coming back to take over."

"You didn't want to come back at all?"

Trey shook his head. "I agreed to do it only if they'd sell the chain, and they agreed to sell the chain only if it would maintain its integrity and identity. So that's what I've been working on ever since."

"Quietly."

"*Very* quietly, because once talk of a potential deal gets out, it's pretty much sure to fall through. In fact, I hadn't talked to Ross at all about it, because I didn't think he'd be interested and I didn't want to tip my hand that the stores might be for sale. Then he approached me the other day at the food court."

Darcy remembered. "*That* was an offer to buy? When he said that you should get together for a chat sometime?"

Trey gave a half smile. "We both danced around it for a while—until the engagement party."

I need to catch Trey for a minute, Ross had told her that night. It had been right there in front of her—except that she hadn't possessed all the pieces she'd needed to put the puzzle together. "I see," she said finally. "So what are you going to do?"

"Go back to practicing law, I suppose. It'll take a while to get myself reestablished after this detour."

"You're an attorney?" She frowned. "Then why did you need Dave?"

"I'm sure he's told you that only a fool tries to be his own lawyer."

"Yeah." She hesitated. "Then you'll be going back east? Philadelphia, right?"

"I suppose so. There's nothing to keep me around here."

It was the answer to a couple of her biggest concerns—at least she wouldn't be running into him at the cottage—but it was also a pain which wrenched her heart. *There's nothing to keep me around here...*

"I'll take care of sorting out the details before I leave," Trey said. "It'll be weeks—maybe a few months—before the merger is complete, anyway."

"At least it's not too late to stop the work on the ring, Trey. The jeweler could still melt it down, couldn't he? I'm sorry—I tried to slow him down by making all those changes, but—"

"Did you really? I told him to go ahead."

What? "That must be why he looked so startled when I butted in."

"No, he was startled because what you suggested was almost exactly what I'd just told him to do. No more amethysts, just a couple of diamonds instead. I told him to use your design—at least most of it."

"But why didn't you stall him longer?"

She thought for a minute he wasn't going to answer, but then he said, "I didn't want to stall him, Darcy. I wanted him to make the ring, I just didn't know why. Not then. Not till this morning, when I found out you'd left this at the store." He reached into his pocket, and suddenly her amethyst ring sparkled in the sunlight falling on his palm.

Darcy felt the sensation of hummingbird wings move to her stomach. "But now you do know? Why, Trey?"

"What is it about women that you always have to have everything explained down to the last inflection?" Trey complained. "Why is it that a woman's favorite question is, 'What did you mean by that?' No, don't even try to answer, or we'll be standing here all day. Because I wanted more, that's why."

"More…what?" she said cautiously.

"I thought you were amusing, and attractive, and cute, and sweet. You were fun to tease, and fun to be with. You were kind to Caroline instead of treating her like some kind of fool just because she'd fallen for an abusive guy. You didn't talk endlessly like my mother did, and so many of the women I've dated. And you bought me yellow socks and made me take myself less seriously."

"I see," Darcy said crisply. "Thanks for explaining. Enjoy the socks."

He went on as if she hadn't spoken. "Then I realized that I was proud to have you beside me, and a bit lonely when you weren't there. And that's when I started thinking about the future—but only a little. I thought I was just playing the game."

"Throwing yourself into the role, for the sake of the public image?"

He nodded. "But really I was scared myself of what I was thinking, so I didn't dwell on it. Because I knew it was going to scare you, too."

He could say that again, Darcy thought. She had only a

glimmer of an idea about what he was trying to say, and she was terrified to let herself believe. What if once more she'd got it all wrong? What if he was about to smash even the last feeble flutter of hope?

"And there was no hurry to think about it, anyway," he went on. "Three months seemed like all the time in the world. It wasn't till this morning, when time ran out, that I really realized what I'd done." He smiled, but the expression looked as though it hurt. "I'd fallen in love with you. Stupid, huh? So here I am. After I did such a good job explaining why I wasn't interested in a real engagement, I suddenly spun round like a compass. And now I suppose if I try to convince you that you want a future with me, you'll be running for the hills."

"You...want a future?" Her throat was dry, her voice crackly. "With me?"

"A future for us, Darcy." He said softly, "You know, I realized as soon as I met you that you were hazardous, but I didn't see what direction the danger was coming from until it was too late. So that's the story."

It was too much. Everything she'd wanted, everything she'd dreamed of...

Darcy didn't know where to begin. She shook her head a little in confusion.

He seemed to take it as a refusal. "It's okay, Darcy. I'll leave you alone now. Don't worry about Ross, I'll fix it." Trey turned away. Hands in his pockets, he sauntered down the sidewalk as if he didn't have a care in the world. And yet there was a slump to his shoulders that she'd never seen before.

She had to do something, and fast—or the man she loved would walk out of her life forever, and he would never know how she felt about him.

She called after him, "So, Trey—are you asking me to have your baby after all?"

Trey stopped in midstride. "Darcy, don't tease me now. I can't take it."

"I'm not teasing."

He turned halfway around.

"Because you can name him Andrew Patrick Kent the Fourth if you want, but you'd better never call him Quatro or you'll have me to deal with."

"Is that a promise?" He sounded dead serious. "That I'll have you to deal with, I mean."

"If you want me," she said, so softly that she wasn't sure he could even hear, "then yes. Because I love you, too."

He covered the ground between them in a few strides, and she went gladly into his arms.

"I love you," he said, and kissed her long and thoroughly.

For an instant, over his shoulder, Darcy thought vaguely that she saw the blinds in the front window of the reception room shift as if someone was peeking out. No surprise there, she thought. She'd only be amazed if Caroline didn't rush back to Dave's office and drag him out to look, too. Then she forgot all about the window and gave herself up to enjoying Trey.

Finally, when he stopped kissing her, she managed to say, "Caroline isn't just working here. She's planning on taking the place over—and Dave as well."

"Why do you think I care what she does?" Trey said against her lips.

"Because now that you have a possible reason to stay in Chicago, I thought you might consider joining Dave's practice, and you should probably know that your sister is—"

"Yeah. Great. I'll think about it later. Right now..." A long time later, he raised his head and said thoughtfully,

"Darcy, if you object so much to Quatro, then how about Rectangle?"

"Absolutely not."

"Hmm." He kissed her again, almost lazily. "Would you consider Ivy?"

"What did you say?" Her brain was feeling like oatmeal. "Who's Ivy?"

He raised a hand and drew the Roman numeral four in the air right in front of her. "I-V."

"A boy called Ivy? *No*, Trey."

"Then I'll have to keep working on it."

"Fine. Only…" She reached up to clasp her hands at the back of his neck. "Don't you have better things to do with your time?"

"Now that you mention it," he whispered, "I can think of lots of them. Let's go inside and discuss it."

Darcy shook her head. "Then we'd have to deal with Caroline and Dave."

"Good point. So let's go home instead."

Home. What a beautiful word it was… "Sold," she said softly, and he led her down the sidewalk to his car.

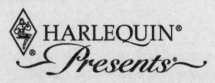

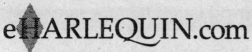

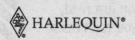
HARLEQUIN ROMANCE®

Coming Next Month

#3859 THE OUTBACK ENGAGEMENT Margaret Way

Darcy McIvor is shocked at the contents of her late father's will.
He's given overall control to Curt Berenger, a man whom Darcy once
nearly married! When her estranged, gold-digging sister returns and
starts making a move on Curt—*her* Curt—Darcy knows that she'll
have to tell him exactly why she ended their affair all those years
ago…or else risk losing him forever.

The McIvor Sisters

#3860 THE BILLIONAIRE'S BRIDE Jackie Braun

When Marnie heads off to the balmy beaches of Mexico it's for
some rest and relaxation. There she meets handsome, mysterious
JT—who makes her *feel* more than she has in a long time. Their
holiday romance is a delicious escape—but can it survive in the real
world? Billionaire JT is determined it will—with Marnie as his bride!

#3861 CONTRACTED: CORPORATE WIFE Jessica Hart

Patrick Farr lives the bachelor life, wining and dining beautiful
women. But how can he make them realize that marriage is
not on the agenda? By marrying his secretary, Louisa Denison,
for convenience! Patrick's proposal would give the single mom the
financial security and companionship she craves. But will their best
attempts to *avoid* love lead them to exactly that…?

9 to 5

#3862 THE MARRIAGE ADVENTURE Hannah Bernard

Why on earth has Maria agreed to do a skydive? She blames
her stubborn pride—and her need to get the better of Eddie, who'll
be jumping with her. Fearless, adventurous Eddie. Her first crush.
The one who'd brushed her off, years ago, saying she was just a
kid. Now, Eddie can't help but notice Maria is all grown up. Will
she take the jump—out of the plane…and into a life together?